jim thompson

the alcoholics

James Meyers Thompson was born in Anadarko, Oklahoma, in 1906. He began writing fiction at a very young age, selling his first story to *True Detective* when he was only fourteen. In all, Jim Thompson wrote twenty-nine novels and two screenplays (for the Stanley Kubrick films *The Killing* and *Paths of Glory*). Films based on his novels include: *Coup de Torchon (Pop. 1280), Serie Noire (A Hell of a Woman), The Getaway, The Killer Inside Me, The Grifters*, and *After Dark, My Sweet.* A biography of Jim Thompson will be published by Knopf.

Also by Jim Thompson, available from Vintage Books

After Dark, My Sweet

The Criminal

The Getaway

The Grifters

A Hell of a Woman

The Killer Inside Me

Nothing More Than Murder

Pop. 1280

Recoil

Savage Night

A Swell-Looking Babe

Wild Town

the
alcoholics

the alcoholics

jim thompson

VINTAGE CRIME / **BLACK LIZARD**

vintage books • a division of random house, inc. • new york

First Vintage Crime/Black Lizard Edition, January 1993

 Published in the United States by Vintage Books, a division of Random House, Inc., New York, and distributed in Canada by Random House of Canada Limited, Toronto. Originally published in slightly different form by Lion in 1953. This edition first published by Creative Arts Book Company, Berkeley, in 1986.

Library of Congress Cataloging-in-Publication Data
Thompson, Jim, 1906–1977.
The alcoholics/by Jim Thompson.—1st Vintage Crime/Black Lizard ed.
p. cm.—(Vintage Crime/Black Lizard)
ISBN 0-679-73313-2
I. Title. II. Series.
PS3539.H6733A79 1993
813′.54—dc20 92-56368 CIP

Manufactured in the United States of America
10 9 8 7 6 5 4

the
alcoholics

His real name was Pasteur Semelweiss Murphy; so naturally he called himself Dr. Peter S. Murphy: rather, his patients and colleagues knew him by that name. In his own mind, he called himself names as hideous and hopeless as the agony of which they were born. *You!*—he would snarl savagely. *You goofy-looking beanpole! You lanky, long-drawn son-of-a-bitch! You scrawny red-haired imbecile!*

Doctor Murphy had always spoken to Doctor Murphy with disparagement and invective. But never with such frequence and intensity as since he had become the proprietor of El Healtho—Modern Treatment For Alcoholics. Not until then had he called himself dishonest; never before, in the endless annals of *Murphy vs. Murphy*, had the defendant been charged with gross incompetence. And yet—and this was odd—the knowledge that he was about to be divorced from El Healtho, no later, barring miracles, than the close of business today, did nothing to modify or mollify the prosecution. On the contrary, tonight he would shut down the sanitarium, and along with everything else, he would stand accused of failure, of bollixing a job, of screwing up the works. *By God, out good!*

El Healtho perches on a cliff overlooking the Pacific in the southerly limits of the city of Los Angeles. It is a rambling stucco and tile structure, styled in that school of architecture known as Spanish Mediterranean to its adherents and "California Gothic" to its detractors; originally the home of a silent motion-picture actor whose taste, whatever else may be said about it, proved considerably better than his voice.

As a matter of fact, it was not particularly unpleasing to the eye—unless that eye were Doctor Murphy's.

His long scrawny shanks clad in a pair of faded-red swim trunks, the good doctor squatted on the beach and stared blindly at the Pacific; April sunlight in his eyes, Arctic ice in his heart. He had been swimming for three hours when a great breaker had caught him up in its arms and hurled him rolling and spinning and half-drowned onto the sand. It had cast him up and out—and it should have, by God; he was enough even to make the ocean puke!—simultaneously burying him beneath a hundred-odd pounds of slithery seaweed.

Lying there, breathless, in the dank tentacled mess, he had remembered those searing lines from—from Wells? Yes, the *Outline of History: "To this stage has civilization progressed from the slime of the tidal beaches . . ."* And there had been a masochistic satisfaction in remembering, in associating the words with his own sorry state.

A hundred million years of life . . . and in what had it resulted? Well, it was obvious, wasn't it? A pile of crap. A will-less thing, floating on the tide, lacking the elementary grace to sink out of sight.

Doctor Murphy had entered the ocean with the intention of drowning himself. He felt that it would be a good idea, a clean-cut scientific approach to an otherwise insoluble problem; and a secret voice had advised him that here was triumph, not surrender, not exit but ingress. He was not sure of the soundness of his hunch, nor the veracity of the voice. Perhaps it would not have been a good idea; perhaps his voyage would have terminated in the phosphorescent muck of the ocean bottom. But—well, that was the point, you see. The fact that he *wasn't* sure. How in hell could a man know whether his ideas were good if he never tried them out?

And if a man wasn't willing to act on his ideas—if he didn't have the guts to act on 'em—why in the hell did he have to keep having 'em?

"Just once"—he spoke to the Pacific, his blue eyes frosty. "If I could just once, for once in my goddam life . . ."

Life had teased and taunted Doctor Murphy severely. It had constantly confronted him with problems, then presented him with solutions—a single solution to each—which he was incapable of using.

It had begun this evil teasing years before, long before he became Dr. Peter S. Murphy and was merely a freckle-faced brat—ol' Doc Murphy's kid, Pasty. Even then, life was giving him problems and answers—that's-the-only-way answers—leaving the rest of the world undisturbed. Was a dog beaten to death? Life brought the matter immediately to Doc Murphy's kid, advising him exactly what should be done . . . if anything was to be done at all. The other townsfolk were undisturbed; the incident was regrettable, sad, but best forgotten. They were allowed to forget it. But not Pasty Murphy. He had to *do* something—and the one adequate thing, the only thing, he could not do. He could procure the horsewhip, yes; he could find exactly the right place to lie in wait. And he could stand up silently in the darkness, bringing the whip back over his shoulder. But that was all he could do, that was as far as he could go. He could not knock the dog-beater senseless, then beat the dog-beater's rotten ass to the color of eggplant. . . .

Once, while he was interning at Bellevue, Dr. Pasteur Sem—that is, Dr. *Peter S.* Murphy had lined up the most delectable piece in all Manhattan. She was a nurse, and she wasn't selling the stuff, you understand. But she required a great deal of working on. Well, young Doc Murphy had worked on that babe for months; and finally his victory seemed as imminent as it was inevitable. One firm and final move, and the jackpot would be his. So, with twenty dollars saved and another twenty borrowed, he took her to a nightclub. And their waiter—oh, damn his white-tied soul—had shamed and snubbed them unmercifully. He had made Doc look like a cheapskate, a boob, a shrimp, a guy contemptible and unworthy of the prize he sought.

Doc had laid his steak knife on the table, with the tip pointing outward. Casually, he had placed his elbow against the handle. Then, he waited, firmly intending to deprive that waiter permanently of what he himself had, but couldn't use. His opportunity came—and went. In the end, he and the girl slunk out of the nightclub, leaving the waiter triumphant and unharmed.

A couple of hundred yards away, now, around a curve in the beach, a neat blue trailer was parked. Doc turned and looked at it, just as a man leaned out the door and waved to him. Beckoned to him. Doc groaned and cursed.

He did not want to talk to Judson, ex-Navy corpsman, now the night attendant, night nurse, night everything at El Healtho. He didn't want any lectures from Judson, no matter how politely and subtly those lectures were delivered. He considered thumbing his nose at the night man. Why not? Who was the doctor in this place, he or Judson? Then, he stood up and shambled toward the trailer.

Though his night shift was over, and he would necessarily be going to bed in a few minutes, Judson had replaced his white uniform with spotless tan slacks and a short-sleeved sport shirt. Looking at him in his neatness, his cleanliness—looking at the man's chiseled black face with its serene intelligent eyes—Doc felt awkward and dirty and shabby. And somehow shamed. Judson was a Negro. He deserved better than his job. Judson served coffee on a small table set up on the sand. He offered cigarettes, made polite comment on the pleasantness of the morning. Doc waited warily.

"I don't like to mention it, Doctor, but—"

"The hell you don't!" snarled Doctor Murphy. "Well, go on. Get it off your chest!"

Judson looked at him gravely, silently.

The doctor grunted a word of apology. "I know. I talked pretty rough to Rufus, and it was the wrong thing to do. But dammit, Jud, look at the stunts he pulls! If I take my eyes off of him for a minute, he's—well, you know how he is!"

"I know," nodded Judson, "but it's only because he wants to better himself. He's ambitious."

"So he's ambitious," snapped Doc. "He wants to learn. Fine. Why can't he go about it the right way? Why can't he be, uh, well more like you?"

"Probably because he isn't me," Judson suggested pleasantly. "Or are you of the opinion all Negroes are born with equal abilities and receive equal opportunities?"

"Oh, go to hell," said Doc, wearily.

"As a matter of fact," said Judson, "I hadn't intended to say anything about Rufus. I didn't see any need to. I knew you were at least as much disturbed by what you said to him as he was—"

"The hell I was!" lied Doc. "I told him exactly what I should have!"

". . . what I really wanted to talk about was Mr. Van Twyne. Do you think he should be here, Doctor? A pre-frontal lobotomy case?"

"This is an alcoholic sanitarium," said Doctor Murphy. "He's an alcoholic."

"I see."

"Well, he *is*. He's worse than an alcoholic—he's a psychopathic drunk. Any other guy, a guy without dough, would be in the bughouse or Alcatraz for the stunts he's pulled. He's damned lucky that the courts gave him this chance; let him have the pre-frontal instead of—"

"The operation was performed in New York, Doctor."

"That's bad? Where the hell would you go for a pre-frontal?"

"To New York," said Judson. "And I would remain there, afterwards, under the care of the surgeons who performed it. Certainly, I would not allow myself to be transported across the country, a few days later, to an obscure—er—"

Doc's pale, never-tanning face had reddened. "I'm a horse-doctor?" he demanded. "I'm a diploma-mill quack? Why, dammit, if I'd wanted to turn this place into a cure-joint—if I'd been willing to sell silver salts and nux vomica at fifty dollars a shot—I'd be rolling in dough instead of—of—"

"No one," Judson was saying, "has more appreciation for your integrity and what you've tried to do here than I, Doctor. That's why I couldn't undertand . . . will he be with us long?"

"I don't know," Doctor Murphy said, curtly. "What kind of night did he have?"

"Very bad, up until around midnight. Restive. Completely unresponsive to sedation. It was actually painful to watch him. He tried to talk to me, but having had none of the re-training he should have had—"

"Save it! Why didn't you call me?"

"I was on the point of doing so when I discovered the trouble. I took off his sheets, and . . ."

Judson explained. Angry fires danced in the doctor's eyes.

"That clumsy bitch!" he swore.

"Yes," said Judson. "It's hard to understand how a registered nurse could be so clumsy. How anyone who's had the slightest patient training could be."

"Well . . ." The doctor studied him frowning. "You're all wet if you think she's a fake. I checked her references myself."

"I don't doubt that she's R.N., Doctor. I might say, however, that good references are rather easily come by."

"But, I don't— Are you trying to tell me that—"

"Only one thing. People work in places like these for only two reasons: Out of altruism, because, like you, they are genuinely interested in helping the alcoholic—"

"Me? Now, get this," said Doctor Murphy. "If every goddam alcoholic in the world dropped dead tomorrow, it would tickle me pink. I mean it, by God! I hate every damned one of 'em!"

Judson laughed softly. Doctor Murphy glowered at him.

"That's one reason," the Negro continued. "And not, I'm afraid, a very common one. The other? Well, that might be broken down into two reasons. Because they cannot hold jobs elsewhere. Or because the alcoholic sanitarium, with a clientele which shuns publicity, gives them a better than even chance to satisfy abnormal appetites."

"But you surely don't think—"

"Only this, Doctor. Mainly this. That the world being as it is, it is a rather terrible thing to condemn a man like Van Twyne to live in it a helpless idiot."

"Who's condemning him? How do you know he wouldn't be an idiot anyway? The pre-frontal is a hell of a long way from being perfected. It's a last-ditch operation—something you have when there's nothing left to lose. Where do you get that stuff, I'm condemning him?"

Judson shrugged. He picked up the doctor's cup with a polite, "May I?"

Doc swung his hand, palm open, slapping the cup far out into the water.

"How about it?" he raged, kicking back his campstool. "Do you think I like this, any damned stinking part of it? Haven't I sunk a fortune in this place without having a dime left to show for it? Haven't I worked my ass off, with nothing but a high-paid bunch of whiners and incompetents to help me?"

Judson shook his head sympathetically. He was very fond of Doctor Murphy.

"Now, get this," said the doctor, his voice hoarse. "I didn't have Humphrey Van Twyne III flown across country. His family did. I didn't solicit him as a patient. His family had him brought here. I didn't want to treat him here. They—their own family doctor insisted on it. What the hell? Who am I to tell them what to do? What if I did tell them? They'd just dump him in another place."

"I don't think so," said Judson. "I don't think they could."

"You don't think period," said Doctor Murphy. "You don't know what I'm up against. If I don't get—" He broke off the sentence abruptly. Something would turn up. Something had to turn up. He couldn't admit to the cold facts: That he would have to raise fifteen thousand dollars today or go out of business, and that the Van Twynes were the only possible means of raising it.

"I'm the guy who has to do the thinking," he continued. "I have to do the doing. Suppose I'm wrong. Suppose I weigh all the factors in the case and make my decision, and it turns out to be wrong. So what? I'm not infallible. I'm a doctor, not God. Goddammit, I'm not God!"

Judson turned his head and looked up the cliff. He looked back at the doctor, and nodded gravely.

"You are," he said, "so far as he's concerned."

2

While Judson and the doctor debated—the one calm and implacable, the other stubborn and angry—still another person wrestled with the problem represented by Humphrey Van Twyne III. This was Rufus; Rufus, also Negro, the day attendant at El Healtho. Rufus was considerably afraid of Humphrey Van Twyne III—"the man with no brains," as he thought of him.

Being an occupant of Room Four (or simply, Four, as the old-timers called it), the politely anonymous term for the sanitarium's padded cell, the man required a great deal of waiting on. And much of that waiting-on was required of Rufus. And while the man appeared docile enough, Rufus was quite sure that he wasn't. He knew something of the man's history. Even without brains, a person who pursued such whims as biting folks' noses off was, in Rufus' opinion, a decided menace.

He did not show this fear, of course; at least, he hoped he didn't. For a medical man to show fear of a patient would be unseemly, and Rufus definitely was—in his own mind—a fully qualified practitioner. He held doctors' degrees from the West Coast College of Astro-Cosmicology and the Arkansas Institute of Metaphysical Science. He had also done post-graduate work in Swedish massage. In view of these honors and the fact that he *did* "practice medicine"—at every opportunity and despite the most dogged and profane protests—his lack of medical education seemed of no moment whatsoever.

Seated in the kitchen of El Healtho, with two plates of ham and eggs in him and his fourth cup of breakfast coffee before him, Rufus thought about the man in Room Four, unconsciously flexing the muscles in his large chocolate-colored hands. He could, he decided, "take care" of the man if he had to. But he sure hoped he wouldn't have to.

Physical contests with the patients were frowned upon, and Rufus, a devotee of the sciences, opposed them on principle. It was just plumb too bad, he thought ruefully, that Doctor Murphy would not let him "treat" the case.

He had almost got to the day before. All his equipment had been readied; and he had had the man's winding sheets unwrapped to the waist. And then Doctor Murphy had stalked in and asked what in the hell he had thought he was doing.

Rufus had explained—given his diagnosis. He was convinced, he said, that segments of the man's perverted brain remained in his system and were making him restless. Obviously, a series of colonic irrigations was indicated.

Doctor Murphy had kicked over the pan of warm soapy water. He had told Rufus to stick his goddam shitgun (*now wasn't that a pretty name to call a scientific instrument!*) up his own butt. And he had declared that if Rufus didn't stop his silly goddam horsing around (*a pretty way for a doctor to talk!*) he, personally, would kick his, Rufus', goddam ass all the way into Beverly Hills.

Pretty—thought Rufus, gloomily, savoring his coffee. A pretty way for one professional man to address another. Oh, very pretty . . . Then he became aware that Josephine, the cook, was watching him, and he exchanged his downcast manner for one of frowning studiousness. He appealed to Josephine's ever-near hysteria.

Drawing a toy stethoscope from the pocket of his white jacket, he blew through first one end, then the other, then draped them around his neck. Propping his chin up with one hand he slid the other inside his jacket, thus assuming a pose at once Napoleonic and convenient for scratching. Josephine started to giggle.

3

Back in the era surrounding World War I, the General had been prominently mentioned as a vice-presidential candidate.

Back in the days of the roaring 'twenties, he had served as chairman of the board of a hundred-million dollar corporation.

Back in the early 'thirties, three press services and a nation-wide chain of newspapers had quoted his opinion—yes, and his firm belief—that we have but to tighten our belts, my fellow citizens, and place our trust in Almighty God, and we shall emerge from this crisis more strong and triumphant than ever . . .

Back in the early 'forties, the early days of World War II, he had . . .

As a matter of fact, he had done nothing; nothing wrong. Nothing that might not have been excused, even rewarded, at a different time. It was not so much what he had done but when he had done it: The artist, Time, had painted him into a picture of chaos, distorting the nominally normal, concealing virtue and exaggerating defect.

He had been in the public eye for years. He remained in it now, the one figure in the picture that everyone recognized. Through the refracted light of familiarity, he became a symbol for Pearl Harbor, for Bataan, for the Philippines, for the accidental shooting-down of friendly planes. Perhaps the General had extended his lines too far. Perhaps his losses had been too high for the results achieved. Perhaps, and perhaps not. It did not matter. Time spun the wheel, and the arrow stopped at the General. He was not merely culpable of one doubtful action or several, but for the whole terrifying tragedy of war.

Just as he had done nothing, nothing wrong, so nothing—nothing really wrong—had been done to him. He was not under arrest on the flight back to Washington. He was not court-martialed. There was no official demand for his resignation. True, there were official news releases to the effect that a detailed study of his conduct was being made and that "proper action would be taken at the proper time." The stories flowed into the newspapers for months—never actually accusatory; only reciting the statistics of lives lost, of men killed and wounded and captured, and stating that the General's responsibility was under study.

The tides of the war changed, and the flow of stories to the newspapers ceased. But the General's case remained "under study," and he remained under suspension, drawing no pay. He asked for a trial. He demanded one. That put him back in the newspapers for a day—in bold-face, front-page "boxes," ironic in tone; in editorial-page cartoons—a be-spurred and drooling idiot shaking a bloody fist beneath the nose of John Q. Public.

But he did not get a trial. Nothing, as has been noted, was ever done to the General.

The war ended. The powers that were turned fretful, annoyed eyes on the General's "case." Restore him to rank? Give him a clean bill of health? Impossible. The public would never accept it. The General himself had become impossible. A common drunk, my dear fellow. Actually! "And did you see the article he wrote for that shoddy magazine? Pure viciousness! Couldn't have got any real money from that outfit . . ."

Somewhere, somehow, in his almost fifty years of military service, a small error had been made in the General's papers. It was so small and so obviously an error, a matter of a *t* struck over a *p* to form the anomalous abbreviation *term.*, that it had been dismissed by everyone, the General included. But, now, when something had to be done with him but nothing to him, the error provided a way out.

The error had occurred in the chronicling of his promotion from captain to major; thus, it affected the higher rank and all other ranks up to his present one. A little confusing? Well, it was a rather confused matter. Briefly, however, it boiled down to this. The *term*, in the papers was—by unanimous agreement—interpreted to mean *temp*. His rank was temporary, in other words; all his ranks had been temporary down to the grade of captain.

Being by age subject to retirement, he was retired without prejudice and with utter propriety at his last permanent rank—upon three-quarters of a captain's monthly stipend. So the case was adjusted, honorably and even with kindness. For, as a person high in authority had pointed out, the beggar managed to stay stiff enough as it was. With more money, he would simply drink himself to death.

. . . This morning, the morning of the day annaled and mayhap analyzed here, he sat on the flagstoned patio of the sanitarium, his steamer chair drawn up close to the sea-side guard rail so that he might better watch Doc's progress up the cliff from the beach. To some, the fact that the doctor chose to scramble perilously and laboriously up the rocks instead of ascending the stairs might have seemed idiotic. But the General did not so regard it. There was very little if anything that Doctor Murphy could do which, in the General's varicosed, broken-celled mind, would be open to criticism.

"A very fine man," the General murmured. "Must remember to—to—to— A very fine man."

Doctor Murphy swung over the guard rail, rested a moment, then moved across the patio, mopping his bony face with a thin wiry arm. He stooped down in front of the General, gently replacing the houseslippers on the chilled bare feet. Then, dragging up a hassock to sit on, he grinned shrewdly but respectfully into the old man's face.

"Short night, eh, General?"

"What?" The General blinked, uncertainly. "Oh, no. No, I slept very well, Doctor."

"Good!" said Doctor Murphy. "You're convinced, then? You've decided I was right about that letter."

"Well, uh . . ." The General fumbled in the pocket of his bathrobe. "I was going to ask . . . I wonder if you'd mind . . ."

Doctor Murphy extricated the letter from the robe, and

carefully unfolded it. "There you are," he said, "right down in black and white. *'We have enjoyed reading your manuscript, and thank you for allowing us to consider it.'* Isn't that what it says? Isn't that what it means? How in the world can you make anything else out of it?"

"Uh . . . you think that isn't a mere formality? That they're only being polite?"

"Ha!" said Doctor Murphy.

"Not their way, eh?" said the General hopefully. "Pretty curt lot on the whole?"

The doctor nodded vigorously. "Any time *those* people say they enjoy something, they mean it!"

"But—uh—they didn't take it . . . ?"

"They were *unable* to. They enjoyed it and they appreciated your sending it to 'em, but—well, you can read it for yourself. *'We are unable to use it at the present time.'* At the *present*, understand? Let 'em wait a while, General. Just hang on to the manuscript; well, perhaps you'd better give it a good working-over, put in those anecdotes you were telling me. Then, send it to 'em and see how fast they snap it up, by golly!"

The General retrieved the letter, and tucked it carefully into his pocket. "I'll do it, Doctor! By George, I'll . . ." His voice faded, and the faint glow in his eyes dimmed. He *would* do it, but—

He coughed nervously, nodding to the serving table at the side of his chair. "As you can see, Doctor, I have just had a hearty breakfast—scrambled eggs, wheat cakes, mil— Confound it sir! What are you smirking about?"

"Sorry, General. You were saying?"

"I was saying, Doctor Murphy, that I had just had a hearty breakfast and that I strongly felt the need for a drink by way of anchorage."

"Now, that's what I like about you, General," said Doc. "That's the trait I like about all alcoholics, the thing that distinguishes them from the common gutter-drunk. They'll try to outwit you, but they'll almost never lie to you."

"I don't—"

"You say you *had* a hearty breakfast. You don't say you *ate* it . . . You didn't, did you, General? Your choice of words wasn't accidental?"

The General smiled, reluctantly. His eyes, straying to the serving table, lit up again. "You're too sharp for me, Doctor. I don't know why I keep trying to deceive you. Now, I don't want to monopolize your time, so if you'll just instruct Rufus to re-fill my cigar lighter I'll . . ."

"What do you intend to do with the fluid?"

"What would one do with it?"

The doctor waited. Now it was lighter fluid. He brought his hands down on his thighs with a weary slap, and stood up. "Arsenic mixes well with milk, too," he said, "and it acts a lot faster. How'll it be if I send you a shot of that?"

"It might," said the General, "be a good idea."

Doc stared down at the bowed head, his friendly concern for the old man mingling with his irritating but ever-absorbing interest in the problem which the man presented. The General's existence was outright defiance of all the known rules of medical science, his existence and that of practically every other patron of El Healtho. Everyone knew that when the alcohol in the bloodstream reached a small fraction of one percent, the person through whom that bloodstream flowed became a corpse. His heart stopped. He smothered. Everyone knew that alcohol rose up the spinal canal to the brain, pressing harder and harder against the fragile cells until they exploded and their owner became an imbecile.

Everyone knew these things. Everyone but the alcoholics.

Of course, they did die. Their brains did become damaged to the point of idiocy. But alcohol, more often than not was only one factor in those deaths and that damage. They were run over while drunk; they were beaten and kicked, with irreparable damage to the brain, in drunken brawls. Everything happened to them except the one thing which a logical science declared should happen.

Of his own personal knowledge, Doctor Murphy had known but one man who had died of alcoholism.

One might justifiably feel that violent death overtook the

alcoholic before his affliction had the opportunity. But how, if that were true, could such elderly alcoholics as the General be explained? The General had drunk a full quart of whiskey in thirty minutes; the alcohol in his bloodstream had been sufficient to ignite (as Doc Murphy had proved) at the touch of a match. Yet he did not die and his health, for his age, was far better than average. His brain was "wet"—at least, important areas of it were wet to an ordinarily disabling extent. Yet he was very, very far from being an idiot.

Doc wondered, and wondered, by God, why he wondered. For, as far as he could see, El Healtho was damned well washed up. He might be wrong; certainly, he intended to take another look at his financial books after breakfast. But, hell, he knew without looking. He'd been looking for months when he should have been out looking for a practice.

Van Twyne? Would his family now take the next cautious step toward the goal which Murphy stood in front of? They would. They would do it today, through the medium of their family physician.

And if El Healtho *was* washed up, if, in short, he *did* intend to tell the Van Twynes and their money to go to hell—if that *was* the case, why had he argued so bitterly with Judson?

Dammit, oh, dammit to hell, anyway! Skip it. Let it ride a while. Here was the General, and the General seemed in favor of a drink of arsenic.

"I'll send it right out to you," he said, "but you'll have to promise you won't vomit it up."

"Excellent," murmured the General, allowing Doc Murphy to assist him from the chair. "Oh, uh, by the way, Doctor. I'm afraid my account may be slightly in arrears . . ."

"Who says so?" demanded the doctor, belligerently. "You telling me how to run my business?"

And then he jumped so suddenly that the General was almost thrown over backwards. For he had heard screams before—he had heard screams that *were* screams. But he had never heard anything like this, the terrifying cry that could only be coming from Room Four.

4

Lucretia Baker, R.N., had had a very good night's sleep. Not in months, not, in fact, since her sudden dismissal from a cerebral palsy case (male) had she slept so well. And she awakened well before six, thoroughly refreshed and relaxed, rejoicing in the apparent certainty of many more such pleasant nights to come. It had been an inspiration to take employment in this place. Not once, during the several weeks of that employment, had a day passed without its delighting interlude. It might be nothing more—*nothing more!*—than an eyelid, twisted beneath a professionally inquiring thumb. Or it might be nothing more than boiling bouillon, forced between lips too weak to protest. But once there had been a hypodermic, driving all the way to the bone, and . . .

And last night!

Ah, last night!

Throwing open the French doors of her room, she stood naked in the cool-gray light of dawn, drinking in the tangy air of the Pacific. She looked out past the balcony and down the cliff, seeing the hunched red-tipped speck that was Doctor Murphy, reveling in the childish, age-old joy of seeing without being seen. In her imagination—a very vivid, much-practiced instrument—she mounted the balustrade of the balcony and called to him, sweetly in the voice of Circe, sweet but imperious, a Salaambo commanding the barbarian. And he came to her, scrambling up the rocks; and suddenly he was there, his feet and hands somehow bound, stretched helplessly on the bed.

She bent over him (in her imagination). She let her full breasts brush back and forth across his face.

"Well," she whispered, "don't you like me? Ith there thumpthing wrong, Doctor?"

She shivered delightedly. The scene changed.

Now, it was she who lay bound and helpless; and it was the doctor who bent over her. And if she was helpless . . . well, if a person was helpless, how could she . . . ? A brief wave of sickness, nausea, swept over her. Her imagination, vivid and much-practiced as it was, would go no further.

She sat down on the bed and lighted a cigarette. She tried to reason with herself, to squeeze out past the door of inhibition which always, when she was on the point of escape, crushed so cruelly and firmly against her . . . A doctor would be all right. Doctors had always been all right. Wasn't it a doctor who had been nice to Mama, all those years when no one else had been nice? Well. There you were. Doctors were different.

Doctors were all right.

She showered in luke-warm water, then turned the cold faucet on full, letting it beat for minutes against the molded curves of buttocks and belly. She took a great many cold showers, and usually they helped; she supposed, anyway, that she might have felt much more unease without them. But even if it had helped this morning, that help fell far short of the aid she needed.

Less than thirty minutes before she had felt relaxed and joyous, ready for anything. Now, there was no joy in her, only the old, never-satisfied hunger, and it was as if she had never rested.

And it was *his* fault! It was always *their* fault! It had been *their* fault with Mama, the mean, wicked, dirty things. *They* had killed Mama—always demanding, and giving nothing in return . . .

Miss Baker dressed in her clean white uniform, her spotless white shoes and stockings. Eyes sparkling strangely, she pinned a white, blue-edged cap upon her brown brushed bright hair.

Last night was just a beginning. It was just a sample of what she would give him. It was *his* fault, and . . .

And why wait until tonight?

In the long hospital day, there is no firm conjunction of one shift with another. Their edges come together raggedly, notably with the ending of the night and the beginning of the day. Feet drag; there is much thoughtful drinking of coffee. Departures are prompt, arrivals late or present only in the flesh. Six o'clock, for all practical purposes, means six-fifteen or six-thirty.

No harm comes of this circumstance. Patients who have not rested well are now fatigued and asleep. Those who have rested are well able to wait upon the satisfaction of their needs and wants. And, naturally, where a real emergency exists, it will be promptly—if sleepily—provided for.

Patient is in convulsions? Oh, God, *another one?* Well, give him paraldehyde—two ounces. Paraldehyde orally, ACTH intravenously.

Patient is in a coma? Caffeine, benzedrine, oxygen.

Patient's heart has stopped? Nicotinic acid. Jab your finger up his butt.

Patient is violent? Hyocsin, restraints.

Then . . . ?

Nothing then. That is all, brother. We can only sprinkle talcum over the cancer. Convulse if you must. Remain in your coma. Let your heart stutter and stop. You won't die, not permanently; only for a few hours, days, a week. The great crazy-colored snakes will coil around you, crawl lazily from your eyes, your ears, and mouth and nose. And you will slide around the wall of your room, clawing, and striking and screaming, and your heart will fail and your eyes glaze and your limbs will stiffen. And you will be dead—but not dead. Only dying. And for such a short time, brother. Think! You need only die this death for a maximum of a week. And then it will all be over . . . until the next time.

. . . But, to return to Lucretia Baker, R.N., the sanitarium was still silent as she crept out of her room. The halls were still empty. She breathed quietly, listening, and heard only the faint, faraway clatter of Josephine and her kitchen utensils. She closed her door without a sound.

There were only three rooms in this wing of the house; her own, the diathermy and X-ray chamber, and Room Four. Moving swiftly down the hall, her footsteps silent on the ribbed rubber matting, she paused briefly in front of a heavy oak door with a single nickeled numeral. Then, she pulled the bolt—there was no lock on the inside—and thrust all her weight against it.

She opened it just enough to allow her to enter; and once inside, she blocked it open with a small wooden door-stop she had brought from her own room. That would allow her to leave quickly—to hear anyone coming up the stairs. And she didn't need to worry about *him*. He *couldn't* call for anyone.

The room was windowless. The walls and floor were of under-padded canvas. The one item of furniture was a low, formica-topped table, its legs bolted to the floor.

He lay on the table, an oval oblong of damp white sheets, held in place by the straps which also held him motionless. Miss Baker inspected the wrappings and was momentarily frightened. Someone had re-done them. That Judson! Would he . . . ? But they wouldn't think that. Why would anyone think that about her?

She looked down at the white-bandaged head, held level with the cocoon of sheets by a stack of pillows. Van Twyne's eyes were open. They looked unblinkingly into hers in a blank uncomprehending stare. Then, they blinked, and something crept up through the blankness.

He recognized her. He knew what she'd done. But he would not remember long; and, at any rate, he was virtually as powerless to speak as a newborn baby.

He *was* a baby, in fact. A big, old mean helpless baby. Couldn't even talk, the nasty, lazy thing!

Terror was crowding into his eyes, stretching the lids, making the whites greater and greater. They rolled in his head, wildly. And his lips moved, his mouth opened and closed—in silence.

Miss Baker laughed merrily.

She took a folded hand-towel from her pocket—oh, yes, yes, she had come well-prepared—and placed it over his mouth. He tried to bite into it, but she knew exactly what to do about that. She gripped his nose between her thumb and forefinger and squeezed the nostrils shut. He began to smother.

"That'll fixth you, you nathty thing!" Miss Baker whispered. "Thtupid, that's what you are! Lazy, bad, thtupid man! Don't even know your own name, do you?"

She had to force herself to remove the gag, to take away her fingers. Tbe sweet agony in her loins was racing to a climax, and in a few more seconds—*oh, thweet heaven, just a few more!*—she would . . . But she did not have those seconds. The mean, stupid thing was strangling.

She looked down at him, all fairness now, her own pleasure merely a necessary potential of a job to be done.

"Tell me your name," she whispered. "If you don't tell me your name, I'll have to . . ." She waited. She lowered the towel. She reached for his nose. "Very well. In that cathe, I have no choice but to . . ."

The smothering began, again. Again Miss Baker's body trembled with a hot orgiastic tide.

"T-tell me"—she panted: she was breathing for both of them—"Tell—me—your—name . . ."

And the billion uncohered images of Van Twyne's subconscious hurled frenziedly against themselves; they struggled upward, seeking a new exit for the one that was strangely absent. They broke through into nothingness, into a patternless uncharted void: just as the exit had been missing, so now was the pattern. Unguided, unrelated, each struggled and shrieked for command; and yet, gradually, a kind of order—a kind of super-chaos—emerged from the chaos—

"Name?" He tried, the images coming from way, way back.

Huh-huh huh-huhwhoooah . . .

"Name?" Name, things, words. And his mind sweating.

Huh-huh-huh-c-a-t, man. C-A-T, Man?

"Name?" A rush, a void, a meaningful meaninglessness.

Huh-huh-huh, sugar, honey, darling, dear, mama's little man nowilayme goddamlilsnob on, daddy DADDY? what you do to me I said so didn't I well who the hell are you think because you're assdeep in dough you can.

"Name?" Everything, everything he ever remembered, mixed up with all the nothing.

Multiply the diameter times pi which gives us well how would you have it if we are to employ the Socratic method the world according to weighs six sextillion four hundred and fifty quintil-

lion short tons andyoucanhaveit brother and if we are to believe the theory of Malthus you'd better talk fast YOU'D BETTER TALK FAST!

"'Name?" The name didn't matter, but something else did.

Humphvan humptydumpty Humphvantwythird. HUMPHREY VAN TWYNE Thir sure, sure you are and I'm Henry the Eighth I'm Mr. God and this is my oldest boy Jesus now let's be reasonable, sergeant, I'm really if I can make a telephone call.

"Name?" It was hot and he had to do something.

Nownownow NOW GET WISE HUMPY BOY. You want to hang onto your machinery, what there is left of it? Well, you'd better start popping off, then, and I'm crapping you negative. You want to leave with

Balls?

Still sore aren't they? That little bitch.

BALLS?

Remember them, all right, don't you? And why not? Ha, ha. How could you forget?

Miss Baker's small body was limp. The fever was gone from her eyes, and her breathing was regular. The sheets were bound tight, terribly tight. Tired but happy, she turned away from the table; stooped to remove the doorstop. And then it happened.

"Balls!" shrieked Humphrey Van Twyne III. "Balls, balls, *BALLS!*"

Miss Baker jumped, bumping her head against the edge of the door. She whirled, panic-stricken, and took a few steps toward the table. She ran toward the door again. What—how *could* he? He was mean, nasty and they'd get her and she hadn't done a thing, only tried to—

He shrieked and kept shrieking, that one terrible word. Shrieked, deafeningly, as though he would never stop.

She snatched up the doorstop, squeezed through the slowly closing door, and ran madly down the hall. She was barely inside her own room, when Doctor Murphy and Rufus, the former in the lead, came pounding up the stairs. She leaned, fearfully, against her door, listening, listening to the sudden starting and stopping of the shrieks, as the door to Room Four was opened and closed.

They'd know, she thought, terrified. *He'd* know. That room was soundproof. He'd know that she'd been in there.

But maybe . . . she'd have to try . . . maybe he wouldn't think of that. *Oh, God, don't let him think of it!*

Minutes passed. *Were they talking about her, deciding what should be done with her?* Then, she heard the door of Room Four open, and she opened her own and stepped firmly out into the hallway.

Rufus bobbed his head as he passed her, carrying a white-enamel hypodermic tray. Doctor Murphy sauntered along behind him, still wearing his bathing trunks.

He smiled at her engagingly. "Some fun, eh?"

"I'm awfully thorry to be late, Doctor, but you thee my alarm didn't go off . . ."

"No harm done," shrugged the doctor. "Wasn't that some yelling, though? Funny. I'd have sworn he didn't have so much as a whisper in him."

"Yeth," said Miss Baker. "'It ith odd, ithn't it?"

"Funny that we could hear him, too. Perhaps the noise leaked out through the ventilating system. Never known it to do it before, but—do you suppose it did, Miss Baker?"

"Well, I thuppoth it—"

"Oh, I forgot. You probably looked in on him for a moment. Didn't you, Miss Baker?"

"Well, I did feel"—*no, no, no!*—"Oh, no thir! I—"

The doctor snapped his fingers. "Of course, not. You were still in bed."

"Well, I, uh—I wasn't in bed, egthackly. I was getting dressed, and—"

Doctor Murphy picked up her right hand. He opened the finger of his left hand, and placed a small square of cambric in her palm, folding her hand around that.

"Must have dropped that," he said, "when you were there—last night."

He grinned at her, started down the stairs. "See me right after breakfast, eh, Miss Baker?"

"Yeth, thir," said Lucretia Baker, her voice a thin whisper. "R-right—right after breakfast, Doctor Murphy."

Doctor Murphy went down the steps to the first landing, turned left down a narrow wrought iron-railed mezzanine, and proceeded to the southernmost wing of the house where his own room was located. He dressed, whistling, feeling unusually pleased with himself.

All his impulses had inclined him to shove Nurse Baker into her room, shake her until her teeth rattled, paddle her little round butt until she couldn't sit down, herd her out of the house and hurl her clothes after her. That was what he had wanted to do, and a man less strong-willed—a man lacking the perfect self-control which he had so definitely demonstrated—would have done *that*. Which, of course, would have been the worst thing he could do.

She was a sick woman: reason had told him that as it cried down the rage that prompted him to smack her. So for once—oh, hell, not just once; he didn't blow up very often—he held onto his temper in the face of genuine outrage.

He had done exactly the right thing.

She was sick. The sick should be cured, not punished. He had taken the first step toward that cure. He had shown the damned nasty little stinker—this sick woman—that he was wise to her goddam—that he was aware of her ailment and yet was not angry with her. He had edged the matter out of the shadowed and secret recesses of her mind. Another such nudge or two, and it would be out in the open. *If* she didn't fly into a defensive rage.

Doctor Murphy carelessly knotted a tie around the neck of his short-sleeved sport shirt, raked his fingers through his hair until it assumed some semblance of order and stuffed a couple of clean handkerchiefs into his pockets. He let his grin fade, deliberately, and stared pugnaciously at himself in the mirror.

Washed up? Who you talking about, bud?

Well? You got fifteen grand in your keister? Anything to keep the bank from tossing you out of here with a few days' grace period?

Now, look. I don't have time to argue with you. I've got work to do, see? I've got to be thinking out something on this sick woman—or is she just a degenerate? I've got all these alcoholics—

Oh, sure, sure. And what the hell's all that going to get you?

What'll it—who the hell said it would get me anything?

Listen, you stupid jerk! Face the facts. Do you want to keep this place going or not? Damned if I know why you would, but do—

You know the answer to that.

Then there's just one thing for you to do. Start thinking about a nice round sum from the Van Twyne farm—

You think I'd do that, just because the family's fed up—afraid to give him the thirty-seventy chance the operation entitles him to? You think I'd keep a man buried here alive, a hopeless imbecile, just because his family is willing to pay for it?

I said I wasn't going to think about it, now, and by God I'm not!

Doctor Murphy gave his image a stern conclusive nod. He turned toward the door. A young man stood there, leaning against the casing, grinning at him.

"Sorry to walk in on you, Doc," he said. "Guess you didn't hear me knock."

"I see," said Doctor Murphy. "And did it occur to you to wait until I did hear you?"

He was, appearances to the contrary, something of a stickler for formality. He liked good manners; except when they were sodden, he usually found those good manners practiced by alcoholics. And this man was very far from sodden. It was unlikely that his system still retained any of the alcohol which had been in it upon his arrival the day before.

The young man chuckled, brushing aside the rebuke. "You've got to fix me up, Doc. Boy, if I don't get a drink fast I'm going to fall apart."

The doctor nodded slowly. He suddenly appeared to be charmed and intrigued by his visitor. "Had quite a bender, eh? Well, I guess when you advertising men hang one on, you really hang it on."

The young man said they did. And how!

"Don't have to worry about your job, eh? If they don't like it at that place, there's plenty of other places that will?"

"Well, I don't want to brag, Doc, but I can tell you this. Drunk *or* sober, I can still do a hell of a lot better than . . ."

He proceeded to brag, while the doctor casually pushed up the sleeve of his hospital bathrobe and took his pulse. He had no doubt that the young man's boasts were true, or almost true. Alcoholics *had* to be good. They lost time from their jobs. They were guilty of disgusting and atrocious acts. Thus, if they were to survive in their professions or jobs, to be tolerated by the world they so frequently outraged, they had to work and think harder than normal people.

So this man probably was very good at his work now. He probably was very much in demand. Five or ten years from now . . . well, that would be another matter. A man's ability availed him nothing if he could not stop drinking long enough to use it. All his talents were worthless if people were afraid to hire him.

"First trip to a sanitarium, Mr.—uh—Sloan?"

"Make it Jeff, Doc . . . Yep, first trip. Usually, you know, I don't want any more after the second or third day. I'm not sick at my stomach exactly; just feel like I've had enough. But this time, I—"

"Uh-huh. I think I understand, Jeff. So I'll tell you what you'll have to do. Get sobered up completely; rest for a couple days until your nerves are straightened out. Then get back to your job, and never take another drink as long as you live."

Jeff Sloan laughed. "You're kidding, Doc. I can handle it. Didn't I tell you this was the first time I—"

"You'll never be able to handle it again. And this won't be the last time."

"But I've *got* to drink. It's part of my job. I have to meet a lot of people and—"

Doc Murphy couldn't decide whether he was angry or sad. A little of both, he guessed. His nose wrinkled, sniffing the air suspiciously.

"Well, I suppose if you must have a drink . . ."

"A big one, Doc!"

"I'll give you an ounce, now. If you want more later, you can have it."

Followed by the young man, he walked down the mezzanine until he came to the padlocked door of a one-time linen closet. He unlocked it and stepped inside. He emerged with a shot-glass full of one hundred-proof bourbon. Jeff Sloan gulped it eagerly. Doc handed him a small ivory-colored pill.

"No," he said, answering the suspicious question in the other's eyes. "It won't make you sick at your stomach. It won't put you to sleep."

Sloan tossed the pill into his mouth. He expressed effusive thanks for the drink, and headed down the hall toward his room. A few steps away, he turned grinning and brushed his hand across his forehead in a gesture of exaggerated dismay.

"Say, that's the real stuff, Doc! What brand is it? Think I'll lay in a few bottles when I get home."

"I'll write it down for you," said Doctor Murphy smoothly.

He re-locked the door of the closet, carefully testing the lock afterwards. He went down the stairs, started to enter the dining room, then turned abruptly in the opposite direction. He had almost forgotten about the General. The old boy had, or had had, a constitution like iron but it was being seriously strained.

The General was lying on a table in a small examination room. Doc took his blood pressure, then, since he had no stethoscope with him, he laid his ear against the old soldier's chest and listened to his heart.

He straightened again, frowning indecisively.

"Well, Doctor. Would you say I was alive?"

"Oh, nothing as bad as that," said the doctor. "I was just wondering what to embalm you with."

"Mmm." The General pursed his lips thoughtfully. "If I might make a suggestion, I believe that one of the time-tested fluids is—"

Doc laughed, tapered the laugh into a severe frown. He

was going to have to stop clowning with the patients, dammit. What the hell was he running, a circus or a sanitarium? It was all right to joke a little, but this incessant gabbing and horsing around was going out the window. As of right now!

He rang the bell for Rufus, stepping out into the hall when he heard the attendant approach.

"The General is pretty run-down," he said, dropping his voice. "How's our plasma holding up?"

"Well—uh—uh—" Rufus started to scratch his head, then quickly dropped his hand as doc's eye caught his. "Why'n't we sock him with insoolim, Doctuh? 'At start 'im to eatin' good."

"Don't think he can take an insulin shock," said the doctor, nodding appreciation for the suggestion. Rufus had plenty on the ball, if he'd only use it. All that had got him sore with Rufus was the latter's bollixing around with that correspondence school crap instead of using his very good common sense. "Guess we'd better make it plasma."

"How about goo-clothes? We 'travenize him, huh, Doctuh? Give him nice goo-clothes brek'fuss—"

"Glucose!" snapped Doctor Murphy. "Can't you remember anything at all? Not goo-clothes, for Christ's sake! Glucose! G-l-u-c-o- —"

"Yes, suh," said Rufus, quickly. "I go get it right away."

"You will not! And stop telling me what to do, dammit! His system won't burn up a good load of glucose, so . . . Oh," he said tiredly. "No plasma? They didn't—wouldn't fill our order?"

"Yes, suh. Sure would stop tradin' with that outfit, if I was you, Doctuh. Ain't a bit dependable no more."

"Yeah. Well . . ."

"Doctuh . . . Maybe—well, me'n General's same type, an'—an' if he wouldn't mind takin' blood from—"

Doc Murphy let out a happy roar. "Mind? Why in hell should he? Why—"

"Why, indeed?" called a reedy voice from the examination chamber. "He would, on the contrary, be delighted, grateful and—uh—flattered."

Rufus beamed. Doctor Murphy clapped him on the back.

"Go on and get breakfast over with—General, you lie there and rest; we'll see you in thirty minutes or so—and . . . Miss Baker down yet?"

"No, suh. She havin' some coffee in her room."

"Good! I mean—uh—well, good."

They walked down the hall together, the doctor apologizing—very handsomely, he felt—for his tirade of the day before. The trouble with Rufus, he declared. was that Rufus couldn't take a joke. Not that Rufus hadn't deserved an A-1 ass-eating, understand, but—but hell!

"Murph!"

"Oh, oh." Doc paused in front of a partly opened door. "Put my breakfast on the table, Rufus. I'll—"

"Murph! Come in here at once, you hideous beast!"

Rufus went on.

Doctor Murphy went in.

He sat down on the edge of the woman's bed, listened to a throaty, tearful and seemingly interminable denunciation of himself, his employees, his hospital, the motion picture industry, the income-tax bureau, the Republicans, the Democrats, the—everything that manic depressive, alcoholic Susan Kenfield could think of—all delivered with beautiful if occasionally inappropriate gestures.

Her hair was snow-white, but her great brown eyes, her face and her body (a considerable area of which was exposed) were those of a woman in her early thirties. At least, one would have to look at her long and closely to suspect that they were not. Just how old she was, Doc could only guess. Probably around forty, he believed, since she had been playing character parts for more than twenty years.

The throaty, perfectly enunciated flood of words began to ebb. Doc patted her affectionately on the bottom.

"Feel better now? Anything else on your mind?"

"Well—well, that perfectly beastly Judson, Murph! I lay here losing my mind for want of sleep, and all I asked for was one teeny nembutal—"

"He couldn't give it to you, Suzy. You were loaded already."

"Well . . . And you, you heartless beast! You didn't even kiss me goodnight!"

"Well, that," said Doctor Murphy, "will never do."

He smacked her soundly on one firm alabaster cheek. He drew away firmly as her arms sought to circle his shoulders.

"Now, I've got to beat it, Suzy. You—"

"Murph . . ."

"Yeah?"

"Murph, lover, you *are* going to help me, aren't you? Oh, darling, I knew I could count on—"

"Jesus Christ!" snarled Doc. "How hammy can you get?"

"Hammy! Are you accusing me . . . You must help me, dearest. I warn you! I'll kill myself! I'll—!"

"With what? There's nothing on the market that would kill an old bag like you. If there was, I'd make you a present of it."

"A b-bag!" Miss Kenfield rolled her great eyes, imploring the heavens to witness this heresy. "This so-called man of mercy calls me a—a—" She choked on the terrible word. Doctor Murphy spoke it for her.

"A bag. Why, goddam you, Suzy, if you weren't so damned heavy I'd toss your tail right out that window!"

"H-heavy," Miss Kenfield wept. "*Heavy!* Oh, y-you fiend! Y-you—"

"Did I get you drunk? Hell, no! I couldn't get you drunk if I wanted to. You were never by God more sober than—"

"You cad! Beast!"

"Did I get you pregnant? No, again. All I've ever got out of you is a big fat headache—yes, all, by God! Your goddamned fees haven't been enough to pay for my aspirin. And yet you've got the guts to come to me and ask for an abortion! You know what you can do, Suzy? Go ——— yourself!"

"I wish I had," sniffled Susan Kenfield.

Doctor Murphy snorted and headed for the door. Reaching the threshold, he paused and wheeled around.

"By the way, Suzy. How far along are you?"

"What's the difference?" Miss Kenfield shrugged. "Two—three months, I guess."

"You guess?"

"I really don't see how it could be more than that, Murph. I mean, well, after all"—she patted her abdomen—"it would have to stick out more, wouldn't it?"

"Mmm." Doc grunted noncommittally, and his eyes swept over her body. Small boned. Compact yet lushly curving. With a frame like that . . . "How long since your last period?"

"Two or three months," said the actress promptly. "I mean, I did *it* about three months ago, but not very good. Not like I usually do it when . . ."

"Uh-huh. I see," the doctor grunted again. At Suzy's age, a women was apt to have irregular periods. In any event, some women had been known to menstruate up to the month they gave birth. "Why did you come to me with this, Suzy? You know your way around. Why come to me with an abortion when you could go to any one of a dozen doctors who would jump at the chance to do the job?"

"But, lover! I—" Miss Kenfield hesitated, and her eyes shifted from the doctor's for the merest fraction of a second. Then, they met his again; brimming with love and trust, wide with innocent honesty. "But why wouldn't I come to you, lover? Why should I go to anyone else when I have my own dearest, darling Murph to—"

Doctor Murphy said a single obscene word, and walked out, slamming the door as Susan Kenfield's endearments changed suddenly to profane yells of reproach.

She was lying; well, not exactly lying, perhaps, but covering up something. Holding back on the facts. That was obvious. But it was also obvious that now was not the moment to get the truth out of her. It would take more time than he had to give at this hour of the day.

He entered the dining room, drew back a chair and sat down at the table and looked at the four patients present.

6

Jeff Sloan, the advertising man, was there, looking decidedly wan and dabbling disinterestedly at his food. Then there was Bernie Edmonds, prematurely gray, preternaturally youthful—somehow spruce and smart-appearing even in bathrobe and pajamas. Not so many years ago, Bernie had won the Pulitzer Prize for international reporting. Not so many years ago, he had been managing editor of a leading New York newspaper, and the author of two best-selling books on world affairs. Now, he was a part-time rewrite man on one of the Los Angeles papers, and there was every indication that he was about to be severed from that position.

Seated on Bernie's right, were the twin Holcomb brothers, John and Gerald. Fifty-ish, plump-ish, bald-ish, the brothers Holcomb owned one of the more successful Hollywood literary agencies—far too successful, in Doctor Murphy's opinion, for their own good. They had become leaders in the field back in the early days of pictures, and long before their alcoholism had reached the point of incapacitating them, the functions of the agency had been delegated to employees whose high pay and equally high degree of competence were legends in the industry. Now G. & J. Holcomb, Inc. (Literary Properties) maintained branch offices in the major cities of the world; and Gerald and John Holcomb—with a six-figure income and no demands on their time—maintained more or less permanent living quarters in El Healtho Sanitarium.

They had been released, after ten days of treatment, early in the current week. Last night, after an absence of less than forty-eight hours, they had returned. Hopelessly, helplessly drunk. Sodden to the gills.

Logically, they should not have been able to get out of bed this morning. They should have been too hung-over and shaky and sick to budge from their room. Yet here they were, feeling quite chipper apparently, and they had actually eaten a considerable part of their breakfast.

Doctor Murphy could only account for their conduct in one way. Turning his head slightly, he called to Rufus.

"Yes, suh?"

"Our friends here"—Doc nodded to the Holcombs—"have some whiskey hidden in their room. See if you can find it."

"Yes, suh."

"Did you hear the man, brother? Whiskey in our room! Now, why would he think that?" It was John Holcomb.

"Why, indeed?" said Gerald Holcomb. "A very rash, impulsive man, if you ask my opinion. Pay him no mind, brother."

"There's something in the atmosphere here," said Bernie Edmonds. "It makes the best of us jumpy. I've noticed it in myself, you know; seem to be very nervous and shaky every time I come here. . . ."

He and the brothers Holcomb discussed this nominal phenomenon, gravely, with Jeff Sloan throwing in an occasional dead-pan gibe.

Doctor Murphy suddenly shoved back his plate.

"Why do you do it?" he said. "That's what I don't get—why the hell you do it! You come here to stop drinking, because you've drunk so much you're goddam near dead. And yet you spend all the time you're in here trying to get a drink. Why? I'm damned if I get it!"

Bernie Edmonds wagged his gray head thoughtfully. "I've never been able to understand it," he said, his tone indicating that the problem was not one of personal concern.

"It's a very interesting question," said Gerald Holcomb, in much the same tone. "Brother and I were discussing it only a night or so ago. You remember, brother?"

"I do indeed," nodded John Holcomb. "I believe we made a mental note to ask our good friend, here, the doctor, about it. But since he seems to be as baffled as we are . . . Mr. Sloan? Do you have an opinion?"

Jeff Sloan shrugged. "The only opinion I have right now is that I'm going to fall apart if I don't have a drink. How about it, Doc, as long as we're on the subject?"

"You've had one," said Doctor Murphy shortly, and he thought: *Dammit, are they all crazy or am I? They act like—*

"Just one, Doc. I only had an ounce. What's an ounce of whiskey for a man with a bad case of shakes?"

"All you need. All you'd better have."

"Well," said Bernie Edmonds, blandly, "every case is different, of course, but my own experience has been that a little whiskey is like a little knowledge—actually dangerous, you know. Less medicative than, uh, aggravative. Aggravative, Holcomb: Is that a good word?"

"If it isn't," said John, "it should be. At any rate, Bernie, I certainly agree with your sentiment."

"A beautiful and concise restatement of an ancient truth," said Gerald. "To wit: A man can't fly on one wing. I believe we're all in agreement, here, Doctor. Mr. Sloan needs and should have another drink."

"Give him one yourself," snapped the doctor. "I know damned well— Did you find it, Rufus?"

"No, suh. Sure ain't no whiskey in that room," said Rufus.

"But—all right," said Doctor Murphy.

"How about it, Doc," said Sloan. "Make it a good shot this time, huh?"

Doc Murphy looked at him. He had given Sloan an antabuse pill, and it takes no great amount of whiskey, in combination with antabuse, to prove damn-near fatal.

"All right," said the doctor. "Rufus, bring Mr. Sloan an ounce and a half of bourbon."

He held out his keys. Rufus took them, returned after a moment with the drink; and Doc carefully returned the keys to his pocket.

"Now, I'm warning you, Sloan. You shouldn't take that drink. You're going to wish you hadn't, and you'd be a lot better off without it."

Jeff Sloan nodded. "I don't doubt you a bit, Doctor," he said, and he swallowed the drink at a gulp.

Doctor Murphy shoved back his chair and stood up.

He strode out of the room and out the front door.

Bernie bowed his head at Sloan in a gesture of appreciation. "Nice going. A very nice act. Doc's thoroughly convinced that you're about to suffer the agonies of the damned."

"And does he love it," grinned Sloan. "I'll have to do some more eye-fluttering and sweating for him. If I play it just right—suffer in just the right amount—I may be able to make him for three or four more shots."

"You're positive you didn't swallow any of the antabuse?" said John Holcomb. "It doesn't take much of it to—"

"You're telling me," said Sloan. "I've had that stuff before. Couldn't sit down. Couldn't lie still. Couldn't get my breath and my heart kept fluttering and stopping. I wasn't sick, you know. Just so damned uncomfortable and uneasy that I wished I could die and get it over with."

"But I thought Doc watched you take it?"

"Oh, I put it in my mouth all right. But I tongued it into my hand when I took my drink."

He demonstrated the trick, while the Holcombs and Bernie looked on admiringly.

Then Gerald glanced meaningfully at John and the two of them glanced at Bernie, and all three stood up.

"If you'll excuse me, Mr. Sloan . . ."

"Oh, sure," said Jeff easily. "You fellows go right ahead. I'm feeling no pain, for the moment."

The brothers murmured appreciation for Sloan's tact and understanding. Bernie Edmonds felt constrained to explain the situation.

"We—the Holcombs, I should say—have less than a quart. As long as you can get it out of Doc, you'd probably better do it."

"Sure," said Sloan. "I'll manage. What about this old guy, the General? I spotted him out on the terrace this morning. Looked like a man who could use a slug, if I ever saw one."

"That's right," said Bernie. "I don't see how we can give the General a drink. He'd wind up by taking the whole bottle and Doc would—well, I don't like to think about what Doc would do. It's too bad, but . . ."

"I understand," Sloan nodded. "Well, I'll see you gentlemen, after a while."

Glowing comfortably from the whiskey, he arose from his chair and sauntered across the room. He stepped through the French doors and out onto a flagstoned patio overlooking the front yard.

Must cost something to maintain a place like this, Sloan thought idly. But for thirty bucks a day—thirty bucks plus extras per patient—Doctor Murphy could doubtless afford it. For that kind of money, he could afford something much better than this; and, Sloan thought critically, keep it up much better.

Of course, the place wasn't filled to capacity, but it wouldn't have to be. Say there were only seven patients, such as was the case now. Well, seven times thirty was two hundred and ten—more than that when you figured extras, but call it two hundred and ten. Two ten times three sixty-five . . . why, hell, it figured out to around eighty grand a year! And if half of that wasn't profit then he, Jeff Sloan, didn't know his tail from a turnip.

His eyes narrowed, suddenly, in a kind of good-natured disgust as he saw the doctor emerge from a clump of shrubbery near the far end of the lawn. He had been down on his hands and knees—a doctor, mind you, crawling on his hands and knees—and he arose holding a bottle. He held it up to the light, shook it, then hurried it away in the direction of the trees.

Then, head down, he came striding up a curving graveled walk to the patio.

Sloan stepped down off the flagstone to meet him.

"Oh, Doctor Murphy. I'd like to talk to you about—"

"Huh!"—the doctor looked up startled, then roughly brushed past the advertising man. "Later. Haven't time for you now."

"Now, just a minute!" said Sloan. "This is—"

"I said I didn't have time, Sloan!"

"But this is important! It—"

"It'll keep then," Doc Murphy flung over his shoulder, and he disappeared through the French doors.

Jeff took an angry stride or two after him; then, red-faced, kicking surlily at the gravel, he moved around the house to the rear terrace.

The good feeling, the sharpness of mind he had know a moment ago, was beginning to leave him. Now he felt shamed, cheap, and, more than that, damned good and sore.

He wasn't drunk, was he? He'd been entirely polite and business-like, hadn't he? Well, then. Where did that bird get off at, treating him like some Spring Street bum?

Moodily, he sat down on the terrace and lighted a cigarette, sat staring out at the ocean. Of course, he had insisted on having whiskey this morning; he'd tricked Murphy into giving him two drinks. But Murphy didn't know he was being tricked, and he'd been pretty tricky himself, and—and, anyway, anyone was apt to need a couple of quick ones when he got up in the morning, and—and the guy had been goddam rude right from the start. If he hadn't tried to throw his weight around, he, Sloan, wouldn't have—might not have—taken even one drink.

Rationalizing, pushing down the unpleasant facts which his subconscious mind sought to present to him, Jeff talked himself into a mood of warm self-righteousness. This Murphy would have to be shown, that was all. Let these other characters take his guff if they wanted to—(*why did they do it, anyway? pretty big people, some of 'em*)—but Jeff Sloan would show him.

Show him, uh, something.

He'd think of something . . . just as soon as he got another drink or two.

He sauntered into the house and down the hall, wonder ing how he could broach the matter to the Holcombs in a way at once polite and insistent. They struck him as being pretty cold fish, if they wanted to be. Bernie Edmonds, too, for all his airy geniality. They were old friends, acquaintances, at least, and he was an outsider, and . . . but surely they wouldn't turn him down. Fact was, they'd already promised to take care of him. They might have done it, hoping he'd refuse—as he had refused—but they had offered, and when he explained why he couldn't hit up the doctor for the time being . . . .

He walked more slowly, hearing the doctor's voice through the open door of a room ahead of him.

". . . all right, General; you just lie here for another hour . . . sit tight, too, Rufus. Don't do any stirring around for the next fifteen minutes . . ."

"Yes, suh."

"Get all that milk down you. Miss Baker, you put plenty of corn syrup in it?"

"Yeth, Doctor."

"Good. Good . . ."

Jeff Sloan came parallel with the door and looked in.

The old boy, the General, was stretched out on the bed with his eyes closed, while Doctor Murphy affixed a bandage to his right arm. Rufus, his body bared to the waist, was slumped forward in a chair, sipping from a glass which Nurse Baker held for him.

The position of her body slightly hiked the white skirt of her uniform, and Sloan got a glimpse of creamy pink flesh. Then, the doctor had turned, and was looking at him with a mixture of emotions in which resignation predominated.

"All right, Sloan. Still after a drink, eh?"

"As a matter of fact," Jeff began coldly . . . *Had he said he wanted a drink? Hadn't he only wanted to discuss a strictly business proposition?*

"Well?"

"As a matter of fact"—Jeff swallowed heavily—"yes."

The doctor frowned. "I don't know how in the hell you're . . . But, okay. Got your keys with you, Miss Baker?"

"Yeth, thir."

"Get Mr. Sloan a drink, then. Give him—uh, well—two ounces, and check his reactions after he takes it. Check him very carefully, understand?"

"Yeth, doctor."

"And I'll see you in my office as soon as you're finished."

"Y-yeth, thir."

Jeff Sloan followed her up the hall, wondering how a trick as cute as this had been allowed to run around loose so long. He considered the possibility of arranging a date for a few days hence, after he was back in circulation. But, intriguing as the idea was, he couldn't really get his mind on it for the moment. He'd have to think about it later, after he'd had—

After he'd demonstrated a thing or two to Doc Murphy.

He watched. fidgeting, while she unlocked the liquor closet and filled a two-ounce glass. He was so anxious for the drink that he almost forgot to simulate the symptoms which the whiskey was supposed to bring on.

He gulped the drink, sighed with relief and shuddered happily. Then, aware suddenly that she was watching him. he remembered, and he staggered and brushed at his brow.

Miss Baker's hand shot out, steadying him. She felt his pulse. She looked up into his face, looked quickly away again, and released his wrist. Turning, she re-locked the liquor closet.

"Feeling all right, Mithter Thloan?"

"Well, not *all right*—exactly, but—"

"Perhapth you'd better lie down a while."

"Well, uh, maybe I had at that."

A trifle worriedly, he watched her round the corner of the hall and head down the stairs. She must have known; he'd have sworn for a moment that she was going to say something. And right at the moment—Murphy didn't have him bulled a bit, understand—but right at the moment . . .

7

Seated in his office, his long legs hooked about the scuffed base of his swivel chair, Doctor Murphy slowly closed the double-entry ledger and shoved it into a drawer of his roll-top desk . . . Well, that, at least, had been one thing he was right about. There wasn't a chance of keeping open without the Van Twyne money—without the fifteen thousand, cash on the line, which only they could and would provide.

He'd been right about that, but it was about the only thing he was right about. As for everything else, he seemed to be off on the wrong foot entirely.

He'd missed a trick with Susan Kenfield, something damned important, obviously, or she wouldn't be covering it up.

The General hadn't responded well to the transfusion.

He hadn't been able to find the Holcombs' whiskey, and Bernie Edmonds, who had been sobering up nicely, would be getting drunk all over again.

Jeff Sloan wasn't reacting as he should to the antabuse, nor—and this could be of even greater importance—to the psychological cold shoulder. Sloan had seemed to need a good hard punch in his ego. He had—it seemed—needed to be shown that a man loses everything, including the respect and consideration of others, in succumbing to alcohol. But what had seemed like a good idea, was, in Jeff's case, apparently a bad one. He'd got angry, stubborn, but in the wrong way.

Instead of getting sore at himself, Sloan was angry with him, Murphy.

Well—Doc Murphy nodded casually as Miss Baker entered the office—he'd have to try another angle . . . if he had the time. Meanwhile, here was an even more serious problem.

She came briskly across the room, and laid the bed charts on the desk, waited, standing, respectfully, as he turned through them.

"Umm"—he looked up and motioned to a chair—"sit down, Miss Baker. I'd like to talk to you about . . . what about Sloan, anyway? How did the drink set with him?"

Lucretia Baker hesitated, fear spreading through her stomach. "It theemed to—uh—stagger him, doctor."

"How about his pulse?"

"Well . . . it didn't theem to be *very* irregular."

"I don't get it," said Doc Murphy. "I just don't get it.

Well"—he shook his head—"we'll have to keep an eye on him. You know there's no antidote for antabuse?"

"Yeth, thir. I know."

Miss Baker had begun to relax. The doctor hadn't said a word about—about anything; he was being just as sweet as anyone could be, and he still trusted her and depended on her. So, doubtless, before it was too late, she had better state her suspicions concerning Mr. Sloan.

"Nurse! Miss Baker!"

"Wha—thir?" said Miss Baker.

He was frowning, almost scowling at her. Obviously, she had been guilty of the one sin which a doctor considers well nigh unforgivable in a nurse: inattention while he is talking.

"I beg your pardon, doctor. I was—was—"

"Skip it," said Doctor Murphy curtly. "I asked you if you weren't on duty yesterday evening when the Holcombs checked in?"

"Yeth, thir," said Miss Baker, a trifle breathlessly. "I checked them in myself."

"That's what I thought. Did you happen to notice the whiskey they brought in with them?"

"Why—of courth, not! If I'd theen—"

"But you didn't thee—*see*—" Doctor Murphy faltered and corrected himself. "You didn't because you didn't stay in the room with them while they undressed. Why not?"

Lucretia Baker dropped her eyes. She couldn't explain why it was possible for her to view a patient undressed, but impossible to watch him undressing.

"I'm thorry, doctor," she said. "I'll be more careful hereafter."

"Well . . ." Doc Murphy took a resolute grip on his temper. "That's about all we can do, I guess. I wouldn't mind so much, if it wasn't for Sloan. It's useless, naturally, to ask them to cooperate with me. After the amount of whiskey he's taken and survived, they wouldn't believe I'd given him antabuse. They'd figure the same as he would that I was just trying to keep him from having a drink . . ."

"Yeth, thir."

"For that matter," fretted the doctor, "if there's any way of scaring an alcoholic out of a drink, I'd like to know what it is. They're scare-proof when it comes to whiskey. You can tell 'em one more drink will stop their clock, but they'll go right ahead and take it. They'll have it no matter how much it costs them. Why we had a patient here—it was a few months before you joined us—who . . ."

His voice trailed off into silence, and he sat staring straight into Miss Baker's eyes—into their thousand-miles-away blankness.

He waited and watched, his thin face tightening with annoyance. And the thought of what she had done was tinder for the fuel of his disappointments and frustrations, a bone-dry fuse needing only one tiny spark to ignite.

A man could only take so much. He—why, a lot of doctors would have pressed criminal charges, but he not only had said and done nothing but was trying to help her. And why? What for? So that she could sit and sleep with her eyes open while he was talking to her?

The spark came.

A full two minutes after he had ceased speaking, Miss Baker's soft lips moved.

"Yeth, thir," she murmured.

Doctor Murphy's eyes flashed. The freckles suddenly stood out on his pale face like so many copper pennies.

"Wha—," said Miss Baker. And then, save for vague gurgling sounds, she was silent. For her chin and jaws were in the grip of Doc Murphy's strong right hand, and her mouth was being forced open.

"Open up!" he said grimly. "Wider! Now stick out your tongue!"

Miss Baker gasped, struggled . . . and went limp. She opened her mouth to its widest and extended her tongue to its utmost.

Doctor Murphy picked up a thin wooden tongue depressor and began probing. Then, as suddenly as he had taken his grip he released it, and tossed the depressor aside.

"There's no reason for you to lisp," he said. "Why do you do it?"

"Why I—I—" Miss Baker scrubbed at her mouth with the back of her hand. "I—"

"Always done it, eh? Well, there might have been a reason for it at one time, but there isn't now. Not the slightest. I'd cut it out if I were you."

Miss Baker nodded. "Y-yeth—"

"Yes! Say it—*yes!"*

"Yes," said the nurse, clearly and firmly.

"There," said Doc Murphy, leaning back in his chair. "See how easy it is? Now watch yourself on that, after this. It's harmless enough in itself, but where there's no reason for it, as in your case, it's a manifestation of something which might not be—uh—desirable. It's a recessive factor. Subconsciously, you're trying to move back into infancy. Look at it this way. Just what did you have back there in infancy, aside from an absence of responsibility? Not much, is it, compared to what you have or could have as an adult?"

Miss Baker's smile was as friendly as his own; more than that: there was something so womanly sweet about it that Doc Murphy felt a pleasant prickling of his scalp.

"Now, I hope I haven't been—"

"You've been wonderful," said Lucretia Baker, softly. "Just wonderful. It's so nithe—*nice* of you to take such an interest in me."

"Forget it," said Doc. "Haven't done anything. Suppose we have another talk, later in the afternoon?"

"Oh, I'd love to!" breathed Miss Baker; and, a little hastily, the doctor dismissed her.

He watched her leave—disturbed, a trifle uneasy, but not unpleasantly so. Judging by her reaction (and what else was there to judge by?) he had managed the interview very well. He had been a little rough, perhaps, at the beginning, but apparently it was just what she needed. Perhaps if he'd got rough years ago with that little nurse at Bellevue . . . and this Baker babe looked a lot like her, come to think of it . . .

Ah, well—Doctor Murphy shook his head in self-reproof—that was out. That had nothing to do with his interest in Lucretia Baker. It damned well couldn't have. He was a pretty free and easy guy—admittedly too free and easy—but he wasn't crazy. And next to diddling a woman patient, there wasn't a surer way for a doctor to jam himself up than to play around with his nurse.

You just couldn't do those things. No more than you could beat a guy with a bullwhip or stab a waiter in the belly.

Meanwhile, as she paused outside the office to collect herself, Miss Baker's thoughts were as confused as the doctor's own. She was no longer fearful; there was no room for fear, with every cell of her brain and body flooded with anger. It was a kind of scatter-gun anger, its main impact diverted somehow from its nominal and original target. There was a shield of authority between it and him, the doctor. Impregnable authority. As yet, at least, he had not given her the ammunition to penetrate it. He had struck painfully into her defenses, inciting her to fury but giving her no focus for it.

"Jutht wait," she promised herself. "Jutht wait and thee what he does . . ."

But it was impossible to wait for that. She had to do something *now*. Right this minute. If she didn't find some way—someone—to . . .

"Yee-ow! Whooo-eee!"

The cry, the yell, rather, came from the kitchen, and it was followed by sundry other wild yells and grunts and shrieks, all mingled with the clamor of crashing cookware and crockery.

Miss Baker's eyes sparkled. Head erect, back straight as a ramrod, she stepped softly out of the office areaway and across the dining room and through the swinging doors to the kitchen.

The peak-tide of cook Josephine's hysteria had passed. Now it was at an ebb, leaving her slumped down on a stool, quaking, shivering and chuckling, her head buried on one arm, the other slowly raising and dropping a frying pan against a shattered mass of one-time plates.

Miss Baker stepped up to her side.

"Jutht what," she said, "ith going on here?"

For a moment, the cook's body was completely motionless. Then, slowly, she looked up, her eyes still red with laughter even as they widened with apprehension.

"I will not put up with thih, Jothephine! Will not, do you underthand? It hath got to thtop!"

"Well, it stopped, ain't it?" Josephine muttered with sullen courage. "I ain't doin' nothin'. You the one that's makin' all the noise."

Miss Baker stiffened. "Look at me, Jothephine!"

Josephine looked; unwillingly, shiftily, at first; then steadily. She looked down into the heart-shaped face, into the wide and clear gray eyes with their silk-soft lashes . . . into gentleness and innocence. And, for the moment, her unreasoning instinctive fear of the nurse gave way to puzzlement.

"How come?" she said—and she so far forgot herself as to scratch her head. "How come you so . . . so mean?"

Mean!

But she wasn't! Never, ever—no matter what anyone said. What they might say *now*. It was a lie, foolish, ridiculous, deliberately hurtful: for the truth was not here in the now of life.

. . . She had been less than three years old when her father died, and he did not exist in her memory as a man; or, more specifically, as *man*. He was protection; he was shelter; he was warmth and comfort and soothing words. But he was not man.

Man was Mr. Leemy.

It was a little more than a year after Your Dear Father's death when she and Mama had gone to live with Mr. Leemy. Mama had explained that the move was *necessary*—how often she had used that word, a kind of Close Sesame: above definition and argument. And then Mama had gone on, in violation of all precedent, to say that they were really very fortunate, to repeat—almost stubbornly, it seemed—that Mr. Leemy was really a very fine man, a splendid man . . . regardless of what people say . . .

And the next day—they moved the next day for Mama had delayed telling her until the last moment—she met Mr. Leemy. And so great was her disappointment that she almost burst out crying.

She did not cry, of course. One didn't cry over things that were *necessary*. She only stood paralyzed, shocked and confused, trying to reconcile *splendid* and *fine* and all the rest with this—with man.

He sat in the dimly-lit library of the house, his two canes hooked over either arm of his chair, the chair drawn up before the stingy coals of the fireplace. He sat crouched, like a spider, it seemed: something that was all bulging torso and puffed fish-white face; his thin pipestem legs tapering spiderishly into shoes that were little larger than her own.

And Mama had dragged her forward, then pushed her a little to the front. And Mr. Leemy had put out one of his puffed, decay-smelling hands and pinched her on the arm.

Involuntarily, she jerked away. "Don'th!" she said.

"Don'th?" Mr. Leemy decided to be amused. "You must be a little boy. That's the way little boys talk."

"No—yeth, thir," she said, taking another step backward, trying to reach Mama's hand.

"Oh, you *are* a little boy, then? That's too bad. I hoped you were a little girl. I like little girls, don't I, Ma—Mrs. Baker? I know what they like, don't I?"

Mama murmured indistinctly. Mr. Leemy tried to pinch her again—and failed; and his teasing became edged.

"Little boy," he said. "That's the way little boys talk. Too bad. Yes, sir, it's certainly too bad you aren't a little girl. I like little girls and little girls like me. Don't you want to be a little girl so . . . ?"

And at last, at merciful last, Mama had said, "I'm afraid the child's a little overwrought. Say good-night to Mr. Leemy, darling."

"I'll bet she can't even say good-night," he said. "You can't say it like a little girl, can you?"

And Mama was starting to pull her away, by then, but

she took the time to answer. She had to convince him. She had to make sure that he would not like her . . . as he liked little girls.

"No, thir," she said. "Good-nighthe."

. . . Thereafter, she had had very little contact with Mr. Leemy. The house was large and there was only Mama, the housekeeper, to do the work; so there was always something to be done, by way of helping Mama, in some part of the house where he was not. Mr. Leemy took his meals on a tray, in his room or the library. She and Mama ate alone. She was sent to bed early, in her own room, and she was made to understand that, once there, it was *necessary* to stay. Mr. Leemy, because of his legs, occupied a downstairs bedroom.

So they saw very little of each other. Sometimes she was almost able to persuade herself that he didn't exist. Sometimes, that is, in those few years before she entered school. Never after that. There were whisperings and snickerings and frank questions about bogey men. (*"He'll getcha, I bet. My mama oughta know, I guess, an' she says . . ."* The teachers looked at her peculiarly, often with distaste, more often and more hateful to bear with pity. And once at recess, when she was coming up the stairs from the girls' basement, she heard a group of teachers talking on the landing above. Talking about Mama and Mr. Leemy . . .

Almost three months passed before she ascertained the truth for herself, the false and ugly truth of adulthood, as opposed to the sparkling and wholly splendid truth of her infancy. Three months of thinking and preparing herelf, of waiting on a necessity so urgent as to outweigh the prohibition against leaving her room at night.

It came: the compelling excuse she had waited for. It came, yet she continued to wait for a few nights, until a night when she heard a soft creaking of the stair treads and, a moment or two later, the squeaking rattle of the library doors as they rolled open and shut again. She waited nearly ten minutes—some four hundred heart beats. Then, noting that she was slightly feverish—and she actually was, she had been so for several days—and that her water glass was empty, she went quietly down the stairs and into the kitchen and drew a drink from the tap.

She had had to get the drink of water. And, as a person incipiently ill, it was certainly wise to pause midway on the long, steep flight of stairs; to sit down and rest for a . . . for as long as was necessary.

She had polished the library transom no later than yesterday, doing it well as she did everything. The spotless glass seemed to magnify the bloated body of Mr. Leemy, seated as always before his stingy fire. It framed him, as in a picture, its oblong outline thrusting him into prominence even as it thrust everything outside its periphery into oblivion.

She could not see Mama. Her head swayed and her eyes drooped shut for a moment. When she opened them again, Mr. Leemy was hoisting himself from the chair with his canes.

He was standing, and her view of him was cut off at the waist.

He braced himself with one cane, and lifted the other.

And she still could not see Mama, but she could him—see the slick wetness of his mouth, his glazed eyes, as he slashed with the cane at . . . at . . .

Whatever was there on the floor.

She could see the cane swing up and down, jerkily. Faster and faster . . .

That should have been enough. The thought that it must be, that there could be nothing more after this—that in surviving this she had survived all—was her sole anchor in sanity during her remaining years in Mr. Leemy's house.

If it had been all, perhaps . . But it wasn't. There was one final bit of evidence in the damning case against man. And this, probably, was the worst of all; because it stripped all those years of meaning. It handed out shame and ugliness, exacted unquestioning submission and exchanged futility. No time of peace. No comfort and security, all the sweeter for past sacrifice and hardship.

Yes, Mama was Mr. Leemy's sole heir, as he had promised she would be, but his estate had never been the vast abundance that everyone supposed, and at the time of his death it was worse than worthless. He had lived it up, as the saying is. There were large, unpaid bills. Even the house and its furnishings were mortgaged to the hilt.

She and Mama had been allowed to move into an old tenant shack at the rear of the main house, and the Doctors Warfield—Old Will and Young Will—the only people in town who had ever been nice to her and Mama—the doctors treated Mama for nothing and gave her, Lucretia, some after-school work at their office (and paid her twice what it was worth), and so she had managed to finish high school. A few weeks before Mama died.

That was undoubtedly all for the best, as the doctors said. Mama was losing her mind. There was something incurably wrong with her insides. . . .

. . . Josephine stared at Miss Baker, troubledly, her brow puckered in anxious concern. At the moment she would have given one of her unpaid week's wages for some Long John the Conqueror Root, or, better still, a pinch of goofer dust. If a person ever needed a sprinkling of goofer dust, and needed it *bad* Miss Baker was undoubtedly it.

Miss Baker was plenty mean, all right; she was a pure-evil eye. But, obviously, no one who looked as Miss Baker was looking—so poorly-pale, like some poor scared-sick chil'—could be responsible for her affliction. Plenty of folks had the evil eye put on 'em. Plain nice folks, they were, but someone made conjure against 'em and from then on, and until the hex was removed, well, those folks was in a bad way.

Rather gingerly, Josephine touched Miss Baker's arm. She was mightily afraid, but it was one's bounden duty to assist innocent sufferers from the evil eye.

She touched the nurse's arm more firmly, then gently grasped her by the elbow and lowered her to the stool.

"You be all right," she said. "You gonna be all right, now, Miz Baker. You drink some nice, hot coffee."

Miss Baker looked blankly down at the cup.

She took a scalding sip of coffee, and her eyes began to clear. Very pleasant, but it must be getting quite late. She would have to get dressed and something—something would have to be done with her hair. It . . . well, it seemed to be pulling, there at the back of her neck, and—it *was* pulling!

Irritably, she brushed at it.

Her hand came down on Josephine's. It almost struck the knife with which Josephine had been about to remove a lock of hair.

The coffee cup dropped from her startled fingers and into her lap. She jumped to her feet, screaming and streaming.

"What are you doing? What were you doing to me!"

"Nothin'," said Josephine, seeing that the eye had reassumed its wicked reign. "Wasn't doin' nothin'," she said, backing away. "No, ma'am, not me!"

"You were, too! Don't you suppose I—What are you holding behind you?"

"Me? You mean me, Miz Baker?"

"Jothephine! Let me thee your handth!"

Josephine shrugged, her lower lip pushed out in injured innocence. She brought her hands around in front of her, and held them out.

"Aw, right," she mumbled, "you like to see han's, there they is. Just plain ol' han's, seems like to me, but I ain't arguin'. Don't make me no min'. I just soon—"

"That," said Miss Baker, her cheeks crimsoning, "will be juth about enough, Jothephine! You *were* doing thumthing to—"

"I don't argue about nothin'," said Josephine. "I show you my feets, you want to see 'em. All I ask is you stan' right there so's 'at coffee runs down on your shoes 'stead of my floor, an'—"

Miss Baker looked down at her ruined uniform. She fled out of the kitchen and up the stairs.

Sorrowfully, for success had been in her grasp, Josephine reached behind her and removed the knife from its improvised holster of apron strings. Holding it to her mouth, she breathed a cleansing film of moisture onto the blade and polished it against her bosom. She took meat from the refrigerator, and began slicing it for lunch.

Josephine sighed, her thoughts moving from the apparently hopeless project represented by Miss Baker, to the incredible density of Doctor Murphy's mind. To the latest proof of that density. The condition of Susan Kenfield.

That was somethin'—Josephine chuckled sourly—yes, sir, that was really somethin'. She wished Ol' Mam had been with her, peering out through the kitchen serving-window, when they'd brought Miz' Kenfield in. Ol' Man or Granny Blue Gum—Granny who was bat-blind and stone-deaf. Because it helped if you could see and hear, but you didn't really have to. It was mostly the smell that you went by. That smell—and how could folks say it wasn't there just because *they* couldn't smell it?—that didn't tell no lies.

Josephine picked up a slice of meat, stuffed it into her mouth, and chewed reflectively. Maybe . . . huh-uh; her head moved in a silent but positive negative. They'd laugh at her. Didn't want her to laugh, but they were always waiting for a chance to laugh at her. So let 'em find out for themselves. It sure wouldn't be long until they did find out.

Any old time now, Miz' Kenfield would be poppin' that baby.

Bernie Edmonds stepped back from the slightly opened door of the Holcombs' double room, the thumb and forefinger of his right hand curved together in a symbol of success.

"Gone on by," he grinned. "Looks like he was headed for the terrace."

"I thought you were a little brusque with him," said John Holcomb. "Didn't you think so, brother?"

"We-ell," said Gerald Holcomb, "I suppose one might say Bernie was unnecessarily firm, but the young man has been succeeding reasonably well on his own. We don't want to dull his incentive."

"True, oh, very true, brother," said John, "And, of course, we had considerably more whiskey at the time we made our offer." He chuckled and turned to Gerald. "Will you do the honors, brother? I'm afraid I haven't enough left to divide."

"A pleasure, brother," said Gerald.

Rising, he undid the belt of his pajamas and let them drop to his knees, A full pint of whiskey was fastened to the inside of his right thigh with a strip of adhesive tape. He removed the tape, measured half of the whiskey into the glasses which Bernie had taken from beneath the bed, and readjusted the bottle and his pajamas.

They toasted each other.

They were friends. For the moment they were relaxed, comfortable. They were not three but one, and defenses were unnecessary.

John Holcomb lifted one plump buttock from his chair, and rubbed it tenderly. "You get a shot in the tail yesterday, brother? From the nurse, I mean?"

"Did I!" said Gerald. "What about you, Bernie?"

"Huh-uh." Bernie rolled his head. "Doc took care of me. I'll tell you about that nurse . . ."

He proceeded to tell them, his opinion being that no shots should be taken from Miss Baker in a position which prevented one from watching her. "Probably doesn't get enough," he concluded. "One look at a man's ass and she loses control."

The brothers laughed. They raised their glasses again, and again each stole a glance at the remainder of his drink.

There was no thought in any of their minds of complaining to Doctor Murphy about Nurse Baker's roughness. El Healtho was far superior to any of the many other sanitariums they had patronized. Miss Baker, despite the occasional painfulness of her ministrations, was far superior to any of the establishment's previous nurses. Finally, but foremost in importance, was the fact that alcoholics can be even less choosy than beggars; they seem to be born with an abundance of tolerance for the defects of others, and they quickly acquire more. They have to.

"Yes," murmured John Holcomb, absently, "it must be very trying, this dealing with drunks day in and out. Can't really blame a person for getting rough and tough."

"I don't see why a really good man like Doc stays in the game," said Gerald.

"Well"—Bernie Edmonds revolved the whiskey in his glass—"it's a kind of personal thing with Doc, sort of a crusade. You know—you didn't know his father died of the booze?"

"No!" said the brothers.

"That's right. Made quite an impression on Doc, and I can't say that I blame him. The father, he was a doctor, too, and a pretty good one, but he'd been going down hill a long time. Lost all his practice, friends, money, and his wife had given up the ghost and died. Well, so he got on this last big toot, got the whole town down on him but good, and wound up in jail. They didn't know anything about alcoholism in those days, of course. He was just a dammed ornery drunk, so into the jug he went until he snapped out of it. No treatment, no nothing. He'd been in four days when Doc, our boy, that is, fought and begged his way in, and he made such a fuss that they finally called in a doctor. Too late—if it hadn't been too late in the beginning. Doc says they gave him enough morphine to coldcock a cow, and it didn't have any more effect than baking powder. He went right on shaking. Shook himself to death."

"Figuratively speaking, of course?"

"Literally. Ruptured himself inside, according to Doc; even unjointed a number of his bones."

"Well," said John, "if Doc says so it's so. He wouldn't waste time trying to scare an alcoholic."

"It's true, all right. Doc was sore at me when he told me, but I know it wasn't a scare yarn. I've read of similar cases."

John said it was almost enough to make a man swear off reading.

Bernie remarked that it was strange how talking could dry the membranes of a man's throat.

Gerald lowered his pajamas again, emptied the rest of the whiskey into their glasses and shoved the bottle under the bed. They toasted each other. As John lowered his drink, his eyes met his brother's in tentative inquiry. Gerald nodded and took another small sip.

By the way, Bernie . . ."

"Yeah?"

"How—uh—how are things going with you? How's the job?"

"I don't," said Bernie, "think I have one. Can't say that I care, really. It was a pretty lousy job."

"What—uh—" John Holcomb squirmed, and suddenly grimaced with pain. "Damn that woman, anyhow! . . . Uh—brother and I don't want to offend you, but if a small loan—"

Bernie laughed shortly. "You haven't been very successful in offending me in that department. But—I guess not. I'd rather not. I'd rather you didn't tempt me."

"Oh, come, now," said Gerald. "What's a few dollars between—"

"What would I do with it?" said Bernie. "What would I do with a few thousand? The same thing I've always done."

"Not always, Bernie."

"It seems like always. No, thanks very much, Holcombs, but no thanks . . . Now, if you can give me a job—and I don't mean any old job; the kind that doesn't matter whether you screw up or not, and you know it doesn't matter, so . . . Jesus!"—he ploughed his fingers through his gray-white head—"how long it's been since there was anything to do I cared about doing! Since I could feel important. Since I was any place where I didn't feel watched, where even the janitor felt he had the right to smell my breath."

He gulped the rest of his drink, shuddered and hastily lighted a cigarette. He inhaled deeply, exhaled, laughed. "Next week," he said, "East Lynne."

"As I was about to say, Bernie," said John, "brother and I would like very much to have you with us, but it's the agency's policy—and no one regretted more than we the necessity to establish it—it's our policy never to employ alcoholics. Never, no matter who they are."

"Wonderful!" chuckled Bernie Edmonds.

"It's not," said Gerald seriously. "It's simply one of those circumstances, such as you mentioned a moment ago, which *is* a certain way, regardless of whether it should be. Look at it this way. We hire an alcoholic for a responsible position, and he works out fine. We hire a half a dozen and they work out fine. But the seventh one—the seventh does not. In one day he loses us more—and this is no exaggeration, it's happened—more than we can make in a quarter. He loses us more than the other six have earned for us. And we never know when one of the other six, or all of 'em, will pull the same stunt. We just can't take the chance. Brother and I, ourselves, never go near the office when we're drinking."

"Never," John nodded. "That's one reason . . . well, you see our position, Bernie. If we can't trust ourselves—a point concerning which there is not the slightest doubt—how can we trust another alcoholic?"

"Sure," said Bernie. "I was only kidding about the job. I don't know what in hell I'd do around an agency."

"Wait a minute, Bernie!" Gerald stood up. "Brother and I feel very badly about this. Isn't there something we—?"

"Can't think of a thing," said Bernie.

"Why don't you try another book? I'm sure if you can give us something to show around, ten thousand words, say, and an outline, we can get you an interesting advance."

Bernie paused. Several seconds passed, while the brothers watched him anxiously, and then he shook his head.

"What would I write about? I don't do fiction. I'm completely out of touch with the world scene—anyone or any thing that could be built into a book . . . No, I'm afraid not."

"Think it over," urged John. "Don't be in too big a hurry to say no. There must be some way—"

"Is there some way," said Bernie, "to turn the clock back to about 1944? See you at lunch, gentlemen."

He winked at them, and, shoulders thrown back, carpet shoes slip-slapping jauntily, left the room.

Jeff Sloan had had a very bad morning. It might not have seemed so to others, but that has nothing to do with the case. Only the person affected has the right to judge the goodness or badness of his situation. Jeff would have described his as pretty damned lousy.

He'd had one vitamin shot last night—a vitamin shot and something to make him sleep. That was all, and . . . well it was their place to see that he *did* take the antabuse, wasn't it? It was their place to keep him from drinking. That was why he was paying thirty bucks a day. If he had to do it himself, why give *them* anything?

He had come here to get squared away, and they weren't doing a damned thing for him. Just keeping him here. Letting him louse around in a crummy old bathrobe.

He couldn't understand why this place had been recommended so highly, why his employers had insisted on sending him here. By God, he couldn't understand it! It wasn't as if there weren't any other sanitariums for alcoholics. *(And he wasn't a real alcoholic, of course; always'd been able to handle the stuff.)* There were plenty of 'em—places that *guaranteed* to cure you of drinking. And they didn't charge any thirty bucks a day either!

He pulled a chair back into an alcove, for a brisk breeze was sweeping in from the ocean. His robe drawn tightly around him, he hunched down in the chair, his normally good-humored countenance almost laughably peevish.

He would have liked very much to obtain his clothes and check out of El Healtho, but to do so was impractical if not impossible. His employers would doubtless be phoning to inquire about his condition, and if he wasn't here—if he was sufficiently recovered to leave here—they'd expect him back on the job. He wasn't quite up to that yet. Moreover, Doctor Murphy quite likely would refuse to release him.

He pondered this last probability, phrasing it mentally as a situation in which they locked you up in jail and charged you for staying there . . . Could they get away with it? Maybe. Maybe not legally. But you weren't in a very good position to kick up a fuss. Certainly, insisting on his release should not be done except in an extremity.

The whiskey was dying in him. Black doubts—a fearful sense of insecurity he had never known before—edged into his mind. Was he really as good at his job as he'd boasted? Was he any good at all? Or were they just keeping him on out of pity?

He laughed impatiently, irritably. Oh, hell. Everyone knew what Jeff Sloan could do. Ask anyone in the trade, and—But could he keep on doing it? What would he do if he couldn't? He'd never done anything else. He wasn't a copywriter or an artist or an accountant or anything like that. All he knew was how to get his teeth into an idea, and give it the old push—to throw it into 'em and make 'em like it. And—

And he sure hadn't gone over very big around here. First the Doc had brushed him off, and then Bernie and the Holcombs. And that could have been a brush-off from the Kenfield dame. She could have heard him coming, and pulled the sick act to duck him. She and the General, both. Something might have been said like, well, watch out for that Sloan character. He'll bore you in spades.

Jeff mopped his forehead with the sleeve of his robe. This was crazy. He was just feeling low. He was making a lot out of nothing. The thing to do was—was—

Well, why not? What he'd thought about this morning? Murphy acted like one of those don't-give-a-damn guys, like he didn't care whether school kept or not. And a man like that was a good man to talk deal to. If he could just pin him down long enough to make a proposition, get him to set a figure, and then do a little talking and phoning around as soon as he got out of here . . . Well, that would show 'em. It would show Murphy.

If—

But—

The alcoholic's depressed mood pulls him two ways. While it insists that great deeds must be done by way of proving himself, it insidiously resists his doing them. It tells him simultaneously that he must—and can't. That he is certain to fail—but must succeed.

It is a maddening sensation. Jeff, to whom it was new, and who was undergoing a relatively light form of it, was almost at the point of yelling when Rufus came upon him.

Rufus had observed him from a small staircase window, noting with satisfaction that the alcove in which Jeff was sitting would prevent his being seen from almost every other point in the house. Such opportunities seldom came Rufus' way, and he promptly took advantage of this one.

"Mr. Sloan, I believe," he said, with such crispness as he was capable of. "How are you feeling, suh?"

"Why—uh—" Jeff looked at him uncertainly, and half-rose from his chair. "Why, all right, I guess."

"Sit still please. And kin'ly lean back."

Rufus pulled the stethoscope from his pocket, adjusted the ear-pieces and slid the detector inside Jeff's pajamas. He listened gravely, his eyes professionally serious as they stared into Jeff's. He stood back at last and returned the stethoscope to his pocket, his pursed lips and drawn-together brows obviously indicative of disconcerting knowledge.

"Well?" Jeff laughed nervously.

"Your heart always been like that?" said Rufus.

"Like—like what? There's never been anything wrong with my heart that I know of."

Rufus shook his head, searching for some safe but authentic temporization. "Well, now, o' course it could be simple—sympathetic. A reaction to some other condition. Kin'ly open your mouth, suh."

Jeff opened his mouth.

He was a little puzzled. He had thought Rufus only a flunky about the place, a waiter and man of all work, yet here he was assuming the functions of a doctor . . . Would they have an interne around such a place?

Everything about this place was cockeyed. If this guy

didn't seem to act quite right—and Jeff couldn't say why he didn't seem to—well, it was only natural.

Rufus looked down at him, frowning, stroking his chin with one hand.

" 'Magine you're pretty constipated, aren't you, suh?" he said hopefully.

"Not so you could notice it," said Jeff.

" 'Magine your head aches pretty bad, don't it?"

"Well, yes. But, look now—uh—" Jeff hesitated. For a doctor this bird was a little rough in the English department, but—

"Stand up, please."

"But—if you don't mind, I'd—"

"Up!" said Rufus firmly.

Jeff Sloan stood up. Rufus placed a hamlike hand against each side of his head, and began to move them in a gentle push-pull motion.

"Feels better, don't it, suh? Makes it feel kinda nice an' easy."

Jeff, his head wobbling from side to side, backward and forward, agreed that it did feel better.

Rufus' hands pressed tighter. Their motion grew faster. "Jus' relax," he said. "Jus' let it go an' I give you a . . . *'justment!"*

He gave a sudden quick jerk. There was a loud *pop* from the immediate vicinity of Jeff Sloan's neck. He yelled, pulled violently out of Rufus' grasp, and fell back against the house.

"God Almighty," he gasped, his head bent over and slightly to the front of his left shoulder. "Y-you've broken my neck!"

"No, s-suh. No, I ain't, suh." A premonition of impending disaster set Rufus' insides a-tremble. "You jus' ain't let me finish the 'justment, suh, 'at's all. I give it one more teeny-weensie twist, an'—"

"Jesus," he grunted, "how stupid can a guy get! I'm goddam lucky I got a head on my neck at all!"

Jeff glared at him. His head poised at a ludicrous angle, he stamped off the terrace and into the house. Boy, he'd had it! All he needed now was to have some of these jokers give him the horse laugh.

Fortunately—for the physical welfare of anyone who might have encountered him, as well as his pride—he arrived at his room unobserved. He closed the door, placed a chair against it (it had no lock) and sank down on the bed. He started to lie back, and a sharp twinge brought him suddenly upright.

He tried again, on his side. He tried it on the other side. He tried it on his stomach. Groaning, a little desperate, he sat up again.

He managed to light a cigarette, and smoked, moodily, moving the cigarette back and forth to his lips with a wide sweeping motion. He flung it to the floor, cursing, pushed himself up off the bed, and went into the bathroom.

God, he groaned, staring at his lopsidedness in the bathroom mirror, why couldn't he have seen that the guy was a screwball? He knew he was only a flunky, knew he must be, and yet, by God, he'd gone right ahead and . . .

He started to turn on the water, then saw that a hand towel was lying in the sink. He picked it up and—

"Huh!" he gasped, and his head snapped up in surprise. His neck popped again, and he grunted out an "Ouch!" and then he was looking into the mirror again, moving his head to and fro, laughing in sheer delight. It was all right. The damned thing had slipped back into place. That little jump he'd given, when he'd seen what was in the sink . . .

"What do *you* know," he said, tenderly, and lifted it up. "Baby, you *are* a life saver!"

He sniffed it. He sipped, cautiously. He drank and said, "Whuff!" and "Wow!"

A hundred proof, by gosh. A full tumbler—better than half a pint—of hundred proof whiskey.

He drank again, the why of the miracle brushed aside in the urgent need to enjoy it. To hell with why. Who cared about why? It wasn't some kind of crappy trick; it wasn't doped up. It was real honest-to-Hannah whiskey, drinkin' whiskey, and he could feel the old lead flowing back into his pencil already.

"A life saver," murmured Jeff, and he meant it literally.

He sipped at the whiskey until the glass was approximately two-thirds full. Then, he dripped water into it until the level reached the top again. He took another sip, held it in his mouth a moment, savoring it judiciously. He nodded with satisfaction . . . Very shrewd, he thought, congratulating himself on the "discovery"; unaware that the trick was the oldest in the alcoholic's repertoire. You could get that high-proof taste in your mouth, then cut your drink back to its original size; and it was almost impossible to tell that it had been cut. Within reasonable limits, you could have your whiskey and drink it, too.

He carried the glass into the bedroom, pushed the chair more tightly against the door and sat down on the bed again. He sipped and smoked, self-confidence and optimism surging through his body in a nerve-warming, lilting tide. That was one thing about going without a drink for a while. When you did get one, it really did you some good.

He grinned, unconsciously, out of sheer high spirits. Boy, he thought, was I moaning low. And not a reason in the world for it, either. No one had tried to brush him off. Bernie and those other guys were all right. They must have put this whiskey over here for him. Maybe he ought to step over there, and—

But suppose they hadn't done it? Suppose he should thank them, and . . . well, aside from the fact that he didn't have enough to share, that he damned well wasn't going to share, it would be kind of embarrassing—they might think he was needling them about the way they'd acted—if they hadn't given it to him.

Come to think of it, hadn't Bernie mentioned the brand the Holcombs had? . . . He had! And that brand wasn't hundred proof.

This stuff now, this must, if he knew anything at all about whiskey, be some of the sanitarium's stuff.

He hesitated, letting his fingers loosen a little on the glass. And, faintly, from the dining room came the tinkle of the luncheon chimes. He relaxed his grip a little more, and the glass slipped slightly, and abruptly he tightened his fingers again, and jerked the whiskey up to his mouth and took a generous gulp.

There was one good drink left, a little less than a third of a glass. Jeff put it under the bed, against the inside of one of the legs. He jerked the chair away from the door, staggered and righted himself and went out.

Doctor Murphy always ate with his patients, those of them, at least, who were able to get to the dining room. It was often a nuisance to do so—nerve-wracking and time-consuming. But he felt that it was necessary, and worth the effort. Much could be discovered about the condition of a patient by his appetite or lack of it, and his manner of eating. Also, by eating with them, he could still any alcoholic suspicions that he looked down on them or was enjoying better food than they.

With the exception of Susan Kenfield, and, of course, Humphrey Van Twyne, they were all at the table today; even the General was there, very erect and urbane and so shaky that he could hardly get a spoonful of soup to his mouth. Doc Murphy studied him from the corner of his eye. He slipped something into Rufus' hand, and whispered to him. A minute later the General's coffee cup was removed, and another set before him. He drank, and his tremblings quieted, and he began to eat.

Doc sighed, silently. It was all wrong; it was murder. But you had to choose: slow murder or quick starvation. When a man had only one thing to live for, bad though it might be, how could you strip him of it completely?

He dropped the problem and moved on to another, ever-present and always hateful. Money. Mentally, and detesting himself for doing it, he began to add and subtract, divide and multiply, to figure over and over, always arriving at the same hopeless result.

The General? Nothing, next to nothing. No more than enough to take care of his medicines.

Bernie Edmonds? Nothing.

Susan Kenfield? Not now. Suzy was always broke and abysmally in debt after a binge. Not now, and now was all that counted.

The Holcombs? Yes. Right on the dot. They would even be good for a generous loan—which, of course, he couldn't ask for or accept. You couldn't be in debt to an alcoholic whom you had to treat. Inevitably, the debt would influence the treatment.

Jeff Sloane? Yes.

Van Twyne . . . ?

Doctor Murphy's calculations ceased abruptly. He caught Rufus' attention, and whispered to him again. Rufus, who had been hovering about Jeff Sloan with a mixture of curiosity and relief, looked aghast.

"Me, Doctuh? You mean you want *me* to feed 'at—"

"Yes," said Doctor Murphy. "What's the matter? You were anxious enough to fool around up there yesterday."

"Yes, suh, but I wasn't foolin' around his *mouth*."

Doc grimaced. "Go on, now. He's the same as a child—perfectly harmless. How many times do I have to tell you that?"

"Yes, suh. You tell me that, but do you tell *him?*"

Miss Baker started to rise from her chair. "I can do it, Doctor. I'm all—"

"Rufus can do it. I've got some case reports I want you to type up."

"But I can do that, and—"

"Rufus!" snapped Doctor Murphy. "Move!"

"Yes, suh. Right away after a while, suh, Jus' soon as I take care all you—"

"Josephine can do anything that's left to do. Now, get moving."

Rufus moved, his great shoulders slumped in dejection. Miss Baker murmured an inaudible word of apology, and left the table. Frowning, Doc watched her enter the areaway to his office.

He hadn't acted very subtly in the matter, but he'd had to head her off. At any rate, there wasn't much sense in being circuitous now when he was going to have to go straight to the mark this afternoon.

He lighted a cigarette and picked up his coffee cup; glanced casually around the table as he smoked and sipped.

The Holcombs had eaten almost nothing. Which must mean that they were out of whiskey and were retaining their inner glow as long as possible by refraining from eating. Bernie had eaten most of his soup and part of a sandwich. Which must mean, since the Holcombs had been his source of whiskey, that he was resigned to sobering up and getting the agony over with. He was trying to face up to his problem.

Doc was rather pleased with Bernie. Bernie could have remained alcoholically eased for several hours yet, but he had chosen to square away with reality now. Necessity, of course, had helped to dictate the choice; what he would do, if he got hold of more whiskey, was another matter.

But he would get no more. The Holcombs would get no more.

Jeff Sloan . . .

Sloan had taken a few spoonfuls of soup, then sat back and begun smoking. He was sweating and his face was flushed, but otherwise he seemed at ease. There was a sureness about his movements, a kind of arrogant geniality in his manner, which was strangely incompatible in a man who had mixed whiskey with the most violent of alcohol-allergy compounds. Strange. Incredible. But alcoholic behavior had a way of being incredible. Sloan was a super-egoist; he'd keep going as long as he was able to stand up. Which couldn't, of course, be much longer.

Certainly, he couldn't have had any more whiskey. Regardless of his will-to-resist, a very little more and he'd be dead or as near death as a man could be without dying. How he'd managed to get away with what he had, with every sip turning into poison, how he could have made the attempt to move in on the Holcombs (Miss Baker had reported Bernie's brush-off), how a man could fight and beg for something that was killing him—!

Doc put down his coffee cup, and turned slightly in his chair.

"How are you feeling, Sloan?" he said.

"I'm feeling all right," said Jeff. "How are *you* feeling, Murphy?"

The Holcombs turned, as a unit, and stared at him. Bernie frowned, and the General looked a little shocked.

"What's the matter?" Jeff's voice rang loud through the room. "He didn't call me mister, did he? Didn't say how're ya Jeff, did he?"

"That's right," said Doc quickly. "I'm sorry. You're sure you're feeling all right, Jeff? Don't you think you'd better make a stab at your lunch?"

"No," said Jeff.

"Well"—Doc laid his napkin on the table—"If you gentlemen will excuse me . . ."

"Wait a minute," said Jeff. "I want to talk to you."

"Uh-huh. Well, I'm afraid—"

"I don't want any whiskey. That's all you think about, isn't it? All you think I think about. This is business. Want to talk a little business."

"I see. In that case we'd better go into my office, hadn't we?"

"Not necessary. Just want to know what you'll take for this place. Cash on the barrel-head."

Doctor Murphy forced a laugh. "Got a buyer for me? Well, thanks, but I'm afraid I couldn't sell it. After all, what would I do if I didn't have a place for you gentlemen to visit me?"

"You mean," said Jeff, "what would you do for another gravy train?"

He looked around the table, grinning, pleased with his shrewdness, and gradually the grin stiffened and disappeared.

"Just a statement of fact," he said surlily. "Manner of speaking. Couldn't swing it if it wasn't a good deal." He waited. He went on again, stubbornly, sullenly. "Well, it is.

Couldn't help but be. Figure it out yourselves. Not kicking. Glad it is that way. Can't make money where there isn't any to make. Doc can get you guys—guys like us—to shell out fifty bucks a day instead o' thirty, I'm all for it. It's got to be an A-1 racket or I couldn't—"

"That's right," said Doctor Murphy. "Bernie, will you see the General back to his room. I want him to lie down a while."

"Now, wait a minute!" said Jeff. "I'm talk—"

"Yes," said Bernie, "let's wait and see what else Mr. Sloan has to say. Go right ahead, Mr. Sloan, you're doing me a lot of good. A little more of your babble, and I'll be about ready to go on the wagon."

"B-but"—Jeff kicked back his chair, his face suddenly livid. "Think I'm drunk, do you? Well, let me—"

"I hope you are," said Bernie. "I don't see how you could be, but I hope so. I'd hate to think that you were so goddam imbecilic as to believe that—dammit, tell him, Doc!" Bernie's voice choked up with disgust. "How many of us do you ever get any dough out of? How long has it been since I paid you anything?"

"Bernie!" snapped Doc, icily. "You have no right to—"

"Then, I'll tell him. I—"

But Jeff Sloan was not there to tell. He had left the table. He was leaving the room, sick, sober with shame. Hating himself. Hating and despising them as they must hate and despise him.

Why had they let him go on? Why hadn't they shut him up before—?

He had to hate them, to move the smothering shroud of hatred from himself to them.

He closed the door of his room behind him, and almost snatched the drink from under the bed. God! He'd have to get out of here some way. Get to a bar—get back to the apartment with a fifth! If he could just get out of here, he'd show 'em a—

The door crashed open. The drink sailed from his hand, and Doctor Murphy was gripping him by the shoulders, shaking him, yelling at him.

"How much? How much have you had?"

"N-not v-very m—" Jeff couldn't get the words out, not with his teeth rattling like castanets.

Doc released his shoulders, and grabbed his left arm. He jerked up the sleeve, and pressed a thumb against his pulse. "Don't get excited, now! Take it easy. Just tell me how much—how—

"Why, damn you, Sloan!" he breathed. "I've been half off my rocker worrying about you. You've had me going around in circles, wondering how in the hell you were doing it! You took five years off my life, just now and—by God!" he roared. "I ought to murder you, Sloan!"

And then he dropped down on the bed, his head buried in his hands, and rocked and whooped with laughter.

"Got a cigarette on you?" he said.

Jeff Sloan gave him one. Hastily he struck a match and held it.

"Thanks." Doc puffed out a cloud of smoke. "You know I'd have sworn you took that pill. I was sure the boys hadn't given you anything to drink."

"Well"—Jeff hesitated. More than anything else he wanted to play square with Doc—to do nothing that would endanger this wonderful friendliness that had reached down to pull him from outer darkness.

But it would sound so funny, saying he'd found the whiskey in the sink. And he couldn't be positive that the boys hadn't . . .

"Well, let it go," said Doc. "Sit down. . . . How are you feeling, by now? Like to have a good big shot?"

"Gosh, you mean I"—Jeff sat down—"I—uh—guess not."

"Sure you would," said Doc. "You feel like you made a horrible horse's ass of yourself—which you did, of course—and you want a drink to forget it. Well, that's all right. Want it. Just don't take it. . . . Incidentally, what's your attitude toward the booze now? Still think you can handle it?"

"Well, I—it certainly hit me hard this time. The little bit I had this morning. Why, Doc, I can—I've polished off a couple of pints in an—"

"You'll never be able to do it again," said Doctor Murphy.

"Or maybe I should say you'd better not do it unless you're prepared to face much worse situations than you created a while ago. You've crossed the line, as we say in alcoholic circles. You've lost your license to drink. From now on, every drink you take will affect you a little worse than the last one. I tell you that. Bernie or the Holcombs or the General or any other alcoholic will tell you the same thing."

"Why do they drink then?" said Jeff.

"That I don't know. I can point to certain things which are factors in their drinking, but I can't answer the basic questions. I can tell you this: It's ten times harder for a man Bernie's age to stop drinking than it would be for you. . . . Tell me, why do you want to drink anyway?"

Why? Jeff shook his head. "I don't know, exactly, never thought much about it. There's a lot of drinking in my line of work, and well, you get all keyed up and can't let down—or you need a little lift when—"

"No," said Doc. "Those are excuses. They're not the reason. There's only one reason any alcoholic ever drinks. Because he's afraid. I know—I seem to be contradicting myself there. I do know why Bernie and the others keep on drinking, but I don't know the why of that why. What makes them afraid, that is. Why they keep on trying to bolster their courage with whiskey when it does nothing for them any more and does so much against them."

"I don't know, Doc," said Jeff carefully. "Not bragging, but I'm considered a—"

"I know. But whatever you're considered—iron-nerved, a pinch-hitter, a guy who knocks 'em cold and wraps 'em up—it isn't enough for you. You're afraid. You've got to keep showing people. The more you show 'em the more you have to. And when you can't . . ."

"Well, maybe . . ."

"No maybe, Jeff. You're that way. What you have to do is accept the fact—and accept yourself as you are. Right now your fears are illusory; they have no actual basis for existence. But if you keep on drinking, you'll have very real cause for fear. You'll be afraid to meet people, afraid they'll snub you or talk about you. Your work will start slipping, and the more it slips the greater the tendency for it to keep slipping. In short, you'll not only think you're a bum but you'll be one. And with all respect to my patients, I'm not using the word too loosely."

Jeff grinned half-heartedly. "I don't doubt you at all, Doc. I know I certainly acted pretty stupid. But—"

"Yes?"

"Well, it's . . . I don't mean that I'm any stronger or better than these other fellows, but—well, I don't think my own case is quite the—"

"I see," said Doc quietly, fighting down a wild desire to laugh—or weep. It hadn't done any good. It never did. They were intelligent people, and you laid it on the line for 'em. And they listened and nodded, and threw in a word now and then. And when you were through . . . "I see," he repeated. "Bernie Edmonds—they didn't come any better than Bernie. And the General and the Holcombs; you know who they are. All big men, smart men—and they can't handle it. But you can."

"Well, now"—Jeff squirmed—"I didn't say that, Doc. I know I'll certainly have to watch myself from now on, be doggone careful when I drink, but—"

"But you're not an alcoholic. A real alcoholic. You've just been drinking too much, and all you have to do is cut down on it. Well, you could be right. I'll have your clothes brought back to you and you can leave."

"Leave!" Jeff sat up sharply. "B-but—I am a little shaky yet, Doc—"

"Oh, you can fix that," said Doctor Murphy. "Put a few stiff ones under your belt—just enough to get straightened out on, you know—and you'll be all right. But I want you to do me a little favor before you go. I've got a problem I want to discuss with you in confidence, the strictest confidence, understand, and get your advice on. I've been needing to talk it over with someone, but there's no one here but these alcoholics and—"

He shrugged deprecatingly, and stood up. Jeff also arose slowly, his eyes searching the Doctor's face.

"Look, Doc, I'm not—I don't think I've made myself exactly clear—"

"Sure, you have. You're not an alcoholic, and I need to talk this over with a non-alcoholic. Someone whose advice will be unprejudiced and dependable. You don't mind helping me out, do you? It'll only take a few minutes, and then you can leave."

"But—" Jeff still hesitated, trying to discover some vestige of irony in the doctor's countenance or words. There seemed to be none. For that matter, there may well have been none. Certainly, Doctor Murphy knew the futility of trying to convince a man, by any method, against his will.

"All right, Doc," said Jeff. "I don't know—"

"I'll explain," said the doctor, and he led the way out of the room and up the stairs.

They reached the heavy door of Room Four, and Doc pushed. The door swung open, and they stepped in, and—

"Oh, my God," he groaned.

12

Humphrey Van Twyne III still lay motionless in his cocoon of winding sheets, raised slightly off the horizontal now by the tilting upward of the table slab. On the far side of the table, the side furthest from the door, was a small serving stand which Rufus was facing, his back to Humphrey Van Twyne.

The index finger of his left hand was clenched tightly between Van Twyne's teeth.

Doctor Murphy took in the component parts of the picture in one swift glance. Obviously, Rufus had turned toward the serving stand, while he was still giving Van Twyne a bite of food. And Van Twyne had snapped down on his finger, thus holding his hand behind him, holding him helpless.

The big Negro was trembling with strain and fear. Doc stepped swiftly around in front of him, looked reassuringly into the ashen face.

"Have you loose in a moment," he whispered. "How bad has he got you? Into the flesh?"

"D-d-don't think s-so, suh. I j-just r-r-reachin' ovah—"

"Sure. Might have happened to anyone, and you handled it just right. Now, just hang on and—"

Doc turned, wheeled around Jeff, standing wide-eyed and pale, and looked down into Van Twyne's unwinking idiot's eyes. He raised a hand—dropped it again. Useless to pinch his nostrils shut; he could still breathe through his mouth. And his instinctive animal reaction to a seeming attack would be to clamp down on that finger.

Doctor Murphy raised his hand again, his left one, and laid it gently against Van Twyne's head. He began stroking the bandages, softly, soothingly. "Good boy," he murmured. "Good, fine, nice. Good boy, good, good, good . . . Rufus, move back this way as far as you can but don't move your finger. . . . Good, nice, fine, good, good, good boy . . ."

Doc's hand moved up to Van Twyne's forehead, rested there a moment, caressingly, and slid slowly downward until it was lying over the man's eyes. "Good, good boy, sleepy-bye good boy, nice fine good sleepy . . . Rufus . . . a fine good . . . Rufus, this good, good boy has . . . all right, Rufus . . ."

Rufus pulled. His finger slid free, and he staggered forward and went down on his knees. Doc helped him to his feet, stood with an arm hugging the Negro's shoulders as he nodded to Jeff Sloan.

"Rufus showed a great deal of intelligence there," he said quietly. "He analyzed his problem, realized that it was something requiring outside help. He'd rather have done without it, naturally; he'd made a mistake and wound up in an embarrassing and painful position. But he knew what had to be done, and he did it. If he hadn't—if he'd refused to face the facts, and wait for help—he'd have lost a finger. We might even have found him dead up here, bled to death."

Doc examined the finger and saw that the skin, while deeply tooth-marked, was unbroken. He advised antiseptic and a hot-water immersion, helped Rufus through the door with his tray and serving stand, and turned back to Jeff.

"That Rufus"—be grinned fondly—"I blow my top with him on the average of twice a day, but I wouldn't trade him for any two people I've got. He may screw things up, but he never lets you down. He has so very little, but he pours it all out for you and scrapes his insides for more. If you and I did as much with what we have—our opportunities and knowledge and backgrounds—well . . ." Doc shrugged and drew Jeff closer to the table. "This is it," he said. "This is what I wanted to talk to you about."

Jeff's gaze veered away from the expressionless white face, its eyes again wide in an unblinking, unseeing stare. His voice was a barely audible whisper. "W-who is it—he?"

"I think you must have heard of him. He's been out of circulation for some time, but I'm sure you must have heard of him. Humphrey Van Twyne III?"

"Him! But—yeah," said Jeff, his lips curling. "I've heard of that crum!"

"Mmmm. You think he was responsible for what he did then? He was the way he was because he liked it that way. He was just one of the bad guys . . . as a seven-year-old would say of a movie villain?"

"Well, all I know is—" Jeff colored. "I guess maybe he wasn't—"

"He wasn't. Mr. Van Twyne here was simply an alcoholic who refused to admit his malady and who had unlimited funds for indulging it. . . . Ever think how nice it would be, when you had a hangover, if you didn't have to go to work? If you could call up a dame, say, and keep the party going? If you could tell the whole world where to get off and give it a kick in the ass if it didn't move fast enough? Well . . . be glad you weren't able to."

Jeff swallowed, his eyes drawn unwillingly to the thing on the table. "Is he . . . crazy?"

"Oh, no. Being crazy presumes an intelligence, and Van Twyne hasn't any. He probably retains some memory of adult life, but it's doubtful that he relates it to himself. Generally speaking, he's on the mental level of an infant."

"Why"—Jeff nodded—"why do you keep him like that? Is he dangerous?"

"Somewhat. A baby will bite and strike, and a baby of this size could be rather painful. But the danger is mainly to himself. You know. Might masturbate himself raw, or eat his own excrement. Things of that kind."

Jeff shook his head. "What are you going to do with him?"

"That," said Doctor Murphy, "is what I wanted to ask you about. What to do?"

He began to talk, outlining the story of Humphrey Van Twyne and the facts of his own dilemma. He spoke calmly, almost casually, neither ornamenting nor understating the awesome and terrifying facets of the situation. Talking as though the responsibility were not his but Jeff's.

And Jeff listened, moistening his lips, now and then, fine beads of sweat oozing through the pores of his forehead.

"Well, that's it," Doc concluded, and he glanced down into Van Twyne's inscrutable face. "It would be odd if he understood any of that, wouldn't it? Of course, he hasn't had much say-so about his own movements for quite a while; but it would still seem strange. Hearing yourself discussed and disposed of, and having no voice in the matter."

Jeff didn't seem to have heard him. He spoke stubbornly, a little querulously. "He's got nothing to do with me. Hell, he's one guy in a million. There isn't a man in a million who'd wind up in this spot!"

"That's right," Doc agreed. "Very few alcoholics are able to hand it out as long as Humphrey did. They get it handed back to 'em in a way that stops the dishing-out process. Someone kicks their brains out or they get pulled in for drunk-driving or manslaughter or robbery. They burn themselves up in their beds or starve or freeze in some doorway. Or perhaps they wind up in a nut house. But . . . I'm afraid you've got me wrong, Jeff. I'm not trying to frighten you."

"I'll bet!" Jeff grinned weakly.

"I mean it. Alcoholics can't be frightened away from drinking. Their own fear of self, until they can recognize it for the baseless and unreasonable thing it is, is much greater than their fear of anything else. No, you can't frighten 'em, and since you're not one—since you're not immediately concerned with the disease—it would be less than pointless to try to frighten you. . . . I brought you up here for just one reason: to get your idea on what I should do."

"Well"—Jeff hesitated—"there's really no other way?"

"None. And I haven't any more time. Oh, I'd be allowed to hang on a few days and wind things up, but practically speaking this is my last day—unless. I'll have to make my decision by late afternoon, get the money by then, or I'll be out of business."

"And you're sure you can't do anything for this guy if—"

"How could I? It's by no means certain that the men who operated on him, specialists, can do much for him. The question is, ethicalities aside, should he have that chance or should my patients—you've only met a few of the total—have a chance? Frankly, I don't seem to have accomplished much with them. I'm just about as far from the answer to alcoholism as I was in the beginning. But—"

"What makes you so sure, Doc?"

"What?" said Doc, irritably. "I've just got through explaining that—"

He broke off, looking at Jeff. And Jeff grinned back at him, grinned in a way that was at once baffled and serious and glad.

"You know something, Doc? I'm never going to take another drink as long as I live."

Doc blinked, and his mouth twisted wryly. "Well, naturally, I'm glad you recognize the danger. But if I had a dollar for every alcoholic who told me—"

"But I'm *not* going to," said Jeff. "Whether I'm an alcoholic or not—well, I guess I don't like that word very much, so let's just say I'm a guy who can't drink and isn't going to drink."

Doc's heart began to pound. A great smile spread over his bony face.

Just one man! Just to pull one of them back, to know that it hadn't all been wasted. . . . But if you could do it with one . . .

"What made you change your mind, Jeff?"

"I don't know. I know in a way, but I can't quite put it into words. Not now, anyway. Maybe I—you're not going to make me leave this afternoon?"

"You're damned right, I'm not!" vowed Doctor Murphy. "You and I have some more talking to do."

"Well, I think I'd be all right if I left. But I want a chance to talk to the boys, Bernie and the General; fix things up with them for the way I acted at lunch."

Doc started to nod. He caught himself. He had to be sure—as sure as it was possible to be.

"Well, I don't know about that," he said. "After all, Bernie was pretty insulting to you. They all acted pretty lousy for that matter, letting you make a fool of yourself and then bawling you out or giving you the silent treatment. Why should you—?"

Jeff laughed openly.

"You know damned well I should. If I didn't, I'd be all hot and bothered and worried, the same way I've been a hundred other times when—"

Doc's hand came down on his back with a resounding whack.

"Jeff, if you don't make it, then it can't be made! If you don't do it, I think I'll—"

"I'll make it," said Jeff.

"I believe you will! By God, I believe you will . . . Now, let's get out of here and—"

Jeff hesitated. "What about him, Doc?" he said.

And Doc's face went blank for a moment. "Oh," be said, slow. "Yeah . . ."

"Were you leveling with me? Did you really expect me to tell you what to do?"

"I—I don't know," said Doctor Murphy. "But as long as I did ask you . . ."

"I don't know, Doc. I—God, I wouldn't want to say! I mean, whatever you—"

"Yes," said Doc. "I know what you mean."

13

The several case reports had been typed and laid on his desk, but Miss Baker was still sitting at the small typewriting stand when Doctor Murphy entered his office. She sat very erect, her small white-shod feet squarely on the floor, her hands folded neatly in her lap. She looked a little like a shy child in a strange house, placed in one spot and afraid to move out of it.

Doc sat down at his desk and looked through the reports; pretended, rather, to look through them. He already knew their context by heart. He knew that Miss Baker's letter-perfect typing would need no checking. What he did not know was how to begin with her.

He looked up at last, nervously, trying to sound informal and jovial and succeeding largely in sounding brusque. "Well," he said, "no use in sitting there in the corner by yourself."

Miss Baker was on her feet instantly. Then she stood looking at him politely, waiting for further directions.

"Over here," said Doctor Murphy, "I want to talk to you, Miss Baker."

"Yeth, thir," said Miss Baker. "Oh, I'm sorry, *sir*—"

"Now, let's not make a project out of it," said Doc, gruffly. "Just sit down and—uh—relax."

Miss Baker sat down in the chair at the side of his desk, but she did not appear to relax. She sat as she had at the typewriter, starch stiff, hands folded in her lap, her neat sweet features fixed in a small smile of polite wariness.

"Now, Nurse," he said. "I think we're considerably overdue for a talk. The situation here has been, uh, rather unsettled—and it still is. Very unsettled. So I felt that if we were going to get certain matters cleared up . . . make any attempt to clear them up . . . we'd better be getting started."

"Yeth—I mean—"

"Say it," said Doctor Murphy. "I don't expect you to overcome a lifelong trait in a few hours. Just spit it out any way it comes to your mouth and then leave it lay. Don't keep correcting yourself."

Miss Baker murmured, "Yeth, thir."

Doc said, "I don't mean to be—uh—" And Miss Baker said, "Yeth, thir?" And he scowled and fumbled for a cigarette. He lighted it, half-way down its length, and cursed under his breath. He took one puff, and ground it out in the ash tray, grinding it into the metal until it was almost pulverized.

His eyes strayed from the tray, and, as though moved by an unseen magnet, came to rest on Miss Baker's knees, at the exact spot where her knees were exposed by the split of her uniform. Absently, they moved up the uniform, exploring small pink-revealing gaps along the way. They moved on and up, then paused again: pitched temporary camp in the half-hidden environs of two cream-and-peaches, gently undulant mounds. They moved up—they were jerked up, suddenly, by another pair of eyes.

The owner of the eyes raised her hands from her lap, and re-secured the neckline of her uniform. There was prim reproof in the gesture, fear and reproof, yet with it . . . something else. A kind of unconscious invitation, a sort of mocking self-assurance. That's settled—it said—and so are you. That takes care of everything . . .

"Now, Miss Baker," said Doctor Murphy. "As I was about to say . . ."

"Yeth, thir?" Miss Baker slowly crossed her legs.

Oh, she knew, all right. She was scared out of her pants, but she knew what she had, and she was throwing it out at him, knowing damned well that he couldn't do anything any more than . . . than he'd ever done anything. Any more than he could have given that dog-beater what *he* needed, or that waiter or that other nurse. Well, she had his number, all right. She knew she could slap him silly with it, and there wasn't a goddam thing he could do about it. You could lose your license for a hell of a lot less than that.

"Yeth, Doctor?"

"Yes," said Doctor Murphy. "As I was saying. I'm rather short on time, and there's every likelihood that I'm going to have even less so I'd like to get right to the point. I want to know something about you. Your background. Your associates. Your—uh—"

"I thee. Well, I believe there ithn't much to add to the information I've already given you. I—"

"That's not what I mean. I'm talking about your personal life . . . You were an only child? Kept pretty close to home, were you?"

"Yeth," Miss Baker nodded. "You might thay I was . . ."

"How did you get along with such childhood contacts as you had? Were you reasonably well-liked? Did you feel at ease, accepted?"

Miss Baker hesitated. She moved her head in a motion that indicated both yes and no. "Well, thuch friends as I *had*, Doctor . . ."

"I see," said Doctor Murphy. "And those friends, I suppose, included boys?"

"Well . . . Ath many boyth ath girlth . . ."

"Uh-huh," said Doc, and his eyes narrowed slightly. No friends at all? And was that her choice or theirs? Had she, being unable to accept the company of males, tried to rationalize the abnormality by also rejecting females? Well, skip it. Hit the center of the target and the rest would crumble. "You had no childhood sweethearts, Miss Baker?"

"No, thir."

"Have you ever had a date with a young man?"

"No, thir."

"Why not?"

"Well, I juth—well, I thuppoth there wath juth never anyone I cared—"

"Oh, come now," said Doctor Murphy. "We can't be too exacting in these things. People who might not appear too prepossessing at first glance can be very attractive when you get to know them better. All you have to do is give them a chance to let you like them."

There was a small but very disconcerting smile on the

rose-pink lips. She shifted a little in the chair, her legs still crossed, absently arching her breasts, smoothing the uniform over them, before she settled down again.

"Yeth, Doctor?"

"Yes," said Doctor Murphy. "You're not living a normal life. Because you're not—well, when we suppress and ignore our normal instincts too long they become twisted. Permanently twisted, if we don't take decisive counteraction. You're young. You won't have too much of a job on your hands if you tackle it now. So tackle it, Miss Baker, and don't lose any time about it. Will you do that?"

"Well . . . juth how do you mean, Doctor?"

"Men. You know what a man is, don't you?" Doctor Murphy tapped himself on the chest. "I'm one, believe it or not . . . Well, what do you say, then? Let's get started on the job, huh? Will you do that?"

"Well . . . I hardly know how . . ."

"It doesn't matter about hows or whys. Just make yourself available, get out to a show or a lecture or some such thing—and if you handle yourself right—don't act standoffish or cold or frightened—well, the rest will take care of itself. You'll be surprised how easy it will be. Will you try it, just once, even though it does go against your grain? Do it for my sake?"

"Well"—Miss Baker hesitated—"I gueth I *could*."

"Good. That's the spirit."

"What time . . . when would you like to go, Doctor?"

"Oh"—Doctor Murphy shrugged—"Why don't you—*what*? When would *I* like to?"

"Yeth, thir," said Miss Baker demurely. "You did thay *leth*, didn't you? You thaid I should do it for your . . ."

"Why, you"—Doc stammered—"you know damned good and well I—"

His mouth snapped shut, tightened into a thin white line. It was always this way, by God.

"Miss Baker," said Doctor Murphy, "uncross your legs!"

"*Well!*" said Miss Baker, and her own mouth snapped shut. "I'll have you know—"

"You'll do what I tell you, that's what you'll do. You'll sit there until I'm through talking to you, and you will not try any more of the nonsense you pulled a moment ago. Do you understand me, Miss Baker?"

She was frightened, shamed, on the point of tears. But when there is nothing to do but fight, that is what you do. "I understhand I've taken just about all I'm going—"

"Oh, no, you haven't," said Doctor Murphy grimly. "You haven't begun to. Why did you lie to me about Jeff Sloan? Why did you let me go on thinking he'd taken that antabuse, pretend that he was reacting to it, when you knew damned well that he hadn't and wasn't?"

"I didn't thay he—!"

"You did it by implication. You did it deliberately to make me worry—to give me some trouble, as if I didn't have enough already. And why did you do that? I'll tell you. Because of what you'd done. You knew I knew about it, and you were afraid all hell was going to pop. So you screwed me up at what you thought would be your last opportunity."

"I will not," said Miss Baker, starting to rise. "I will not lithen to thuch vulgar—"

"So I'm vulgar, am I? Well, let me tell you what you are. A dirty, sneaky little sadist. Binding that poor helpless bastard's scrotum up in the sheets! Oh, yes you did; I'd hate to think what the poor devil went through before Judson spotted the trouble. And what were you doing in there this morning? Something goddam rotten to make him yell like that! Good God, girl—you can't go on this way! The longer you keep at it the worse you'll get. Sooner or later, you'll do something that—"

"Y-you! *You* having the unsthpeakable nerve to lecture me! A whithkey doctor—a—a—racketeer!"

"Now, wait a minute—!" Doc was outraged by the unfairness of the attack. "Why, damn you, you know I don't—you know this is the one sanitarium where an alcoholic can—"

"Oh, yeth! You're an angel, you are!" Miss Baker's eyes sparkled with malicious triumph. "Well, what about thith poor Mr. Van Twyne that you're tho contherned about?

Thinth when doth a pre-frontal lobotomy cathe belong in a plathe like thith? Where do you get off at—"

"Shut up," said Doctor Murphy.

"I will not thut up! You tharted thith! Now I'm going to—"

"—to shut up," said the doctor. "Now. Immediately. Because if you do not, my dear Lucretia"—he tapped her slowly on the knee, emphasizing each word—"I am going to wallop that sadistic little ass of yours so hard you won't be able to sit down for the next six weeks."

Miss Baker gasped. "Y-you big—"

"Six weeks, Lucretia," said Doctor Murphy. "And don't think I won't love doing it. Now, you were about to say something?"

Miss Baker wasn't about to, apparently. She sat, lips compressed, breast rising and falling in frustrated fury.

Doc nodded, satisfied, and turned to his desk. He wrote out a check and tossed it into her lap.

"You didn't resign," he said. "I fired you. Now pack up your duds and get out of here, and don't take too much time or I'll give you some assistance."

14

Stretched out on the office couch, Doctor Murphy opened one reluctant eye and glanced at his wristwatch. After two o'clock, less than three hours, a little more than two hours and a half, before the Van Twyne's physician, Doctor Perthborg, would arrive. Before his decision would have to be made. And he was as uncertain as to what that decision should be as he had ever been. He just hadn't had time to think it through; there seemed never to be time to think anything through.

Doc sighed and swung his feet to the floor, sat with his elbows on knees staring glumly at the carpet. Judson had the right idea, all right. Not to live in the place. To have certain times for talking and administering to the patients, and, then, barring emergencies, to keep to yourself. Conserve your energies for major problems, that was the idea. Don't chase all to hell over everywhere, dissipating your time on a thousand and one things which, if they needed taking care of at all, could just as well be handled by someone else.

The trouble, Doc decided, entering a new complaint in the case of *Murphy vs. Murphy,* was that he was a goddam know-it-all. He thought he knew everything, and that no one else knew anything. Had to go around sticking his nose in the job, sniffing and scowling and worrying, scolding and asking questions, getting everyone so mixed up they couldn't find their ass with both hands.

Well! If he did decide to hold on here, there was going to be one hell of a change. He'd make a round of the patients in the morning and another in the evening. Meals would be served at certain hours, and no others, and if they didn't eat then they could—

"Damn!" said Doctor Murphy, suddenly, and he leaped up and strode into the kitchen.

Josephine was seated at the kitchen work-table, sipping a cup of coffee before beginning the job of preparing dinner. Her face became noticeably glum at the doctor's appearance, and her greeting was as barren of enthusiasm as a pawnbroker examining a dime-store ring.

"What *you,*" she said, "want *now?*"

"Nothing much"—Doc forced a laugh. "Nothing at all, really. Just a little milk toast and some soft-scrambled eggs—better fry 'em in butter and put just a dash of cayenne in them—and, oh, yes, a pot of hot tea."

Josephine grunted. "Nothin' at all," she mumbled. "Ain't nothin' really at all, 'at ain't. Who it for, anyway?"

"Miss Kenfield," said Doc, and hesitated. "By the way, would you mind taking it to her? Rufus has his hands full with the men patients."

"I got my hands full, too," said Josephine. "How come Miz Baker don' do it?"

"Miss Baker isn't with us any more. She's getting ready to leave."

"Now? She gettin' ready to leave *now?*" Josephine

displayed interest at last. "How come she do 'at?"

"Never mind. If you'll just—"

"You fire her, I bet," said Josephine. "How come you got to do it? You got to do it right now—couldn't wait no little while?"

"I could not," said Doctor Murphy, "and I will not discuss it. Now, please—PLEASE!—fix Miss Kenfield's lunch and take it to her."

"She ain't goin' to eat it, nohow."

"Please," said Doc. "just this once, please do what I ask you without arguing about it."

"Ain't arguin'," said Josephine. "Just tellin' you. She ain't goin' eat it. You want to do 'at woman a favor, doctuh, you give her nice big hot toddy. Hee, hee!" she cackled. " 'At fix her up."

Doctor Murphy glowered helplessly. "All right," he said, "I give up. Just forget the whole thing. I should have known better than to ask. I've never known it to fail, by God—by Christ in heaven, I've never known it to fail! I ask you for some simple little thing and—"

"What you cussin' an' fussin' about? Said I was goin' to do it," said Josephine.

"Well, do it then!"

"Ain't no hurry," Said Josephine. "She ain' goin' to eat it nohow."

Doc turned and stamped out of the kitchen. Josephine's shoulders shook with impish, silent laughter; then, sobering, she looked thoughtfully up at the ceiling.

She was relieved, in a way, that Miss Baker was departing, but, in another sense, troubled and saddened by the fact. She knew the regret that all conscientious people know when they have left unaccomplished some necessary task which they, and they alone, are capable of accomplishing. She had tried, of course, but her effort, upon reflection, appeared pitifully weak. In any event, tryin' wasn't doin' . . . and Miss Baker, unwitting and innocent handmaiden to the evil eye, stood in imperative need of having something done about her. Once she left here, nothing could—rather, would be done. Because no one would *know*. They didn't have the gift of knowin'. So, Miss Baker would continue in her innocently evil way, inevitably suffering the consequences of the wickedness which she could not help but commit. And it all could have been avoided so easily.

It might, Josephine decided resolutely, still be avoided.

She arose from the table, plodded across the floor to the kitchen cabinet and opened a utensil drawer. Scanning its contents thoughtfully, she selected a razor-edged paring-knife and a small, hardwood potato masher. She hefted the last implement, hesitated frowning, then shrugged and dropped it and the knife into the capacious pockets of her apron.

Meanwhile, Doctor Murphy was completing a restless tour of the sanitarium.

He had found the General's room empty, also Jeff Sloan's and Bernie Edmonds'. But judging by the murmur of voices, muted by the closed door of the Holcombs' double room, they were all in there together. And they seemed to be having a very good time for themselves.

It was a circumstance ordinarily to be regarded with considerable suspicion. But Doc could think of no cause for alarm in the present case. It was only natural that Jeff, having offended them all at luncheon, would be gathered into the group with alcoholic wholeheartedness once he had apologized. They never did anything by half-stages, these alcoholics. Hypersensitive themselves, they would not be content with a mere acceptance of Jeff's apologies. They would be in there now, doubtless reciting terrible social misadventures of their own, proving that Jeff's *faux pas* was nothing at all by comparison.

And it was good for them all to be together like this, so long as they didn't have any whiskey, as they naturally didn't. It helped to pass the time, the friendly enemy of alcoholics. It took their mind off of drinking. Anyway, well, Jeff wouldn't be drinking. He wouldn't be in a group that was drinking.

Doc fidgeted indecisively. Then, faintly, he heard a laugh and he grinned with relief and proceeded down the hall. Rufus: there wasn't another person in the world who laughed like that. With Rufus *and* Jeff in there, everything was bound to be all right.

He stopped at Susan Kenfield's door, and knocked. There was a groaned, profane inquiry as to his identity, and he pushed the door open and entered.

Susan Kenfield lay on her stomach, the sheet almost covering her head, her face buried in the pillows. She moaned as Doctor Murphy sat down on the edge of the bed, then, turning slowly, she pushed herself up with her hands and sat up.

"Dying, she said. "Dying like some poor trapped beast, and never a hand turned to help me. Tortured. Alone. Wracked with pain. Perishing of thirst."

"Umm," said Doc. "I'll get you a drink of water."

"*Water!* What the hell do I want with water?" Miss Kenfield trembled with outrage. "A voice crying in the wilderness. I ask for bread, and he gives me a stone."

"Speaking of bread," said Doctor Murphy. "I'm having Joseephine bring in some lunch. Raw chicken livers with strawberry gravy."

Miss Kenfield gasped. She flung her hands over her mouth and bent forward, her body jerking convulsively.

"You'd better behave," said Doc. "Snap out of it, now, and stop acting like a baby. Josephine's bringing something good—something you'll be able to eat. While we're waiting for it, I want to ask you a few questions."

"Go 'way, Murph," Miss Kenfield groaned. "Just go away and let me die in peace."

"Cut it out, Suzy," Doc scoffed. "Every time you come off a drunk, you think you're going to die. Now—"

"But, Murph! I've never felt this way before! It's as though something were squeezing me—down *there*. I don't know quite how to describe it, but—"

"Uh-huh," Doctor Murphy nodded. "So you're pregnant along with the hangover. You're very much pregnant, Suzy, which is why you're sobering up fast and getting out of here. I'm not an obstetrician. I haven't delivered a baby since I interned, and the nurses handled most of the work then."

Miss Kenfield laughed weakly. "You're trying to frighten me, Murph. Just look at me. Now, you know good and well I couldn't be *that* pregnant!"

"Well," Doc hesitated, his eyes traveling up from the rounded flesh of her abdomen to the lush, over-full breasts. She looked, it seemed to him, no different from usual. No different than she had at the time of her last trip to the sanitarium, three or four months ago. Well, perhaps she was a little heavier—a little bloated—but she'd been on this bat for three weeks, and three weeks of guzzling high-calorie booze. . . .

"You're just mean," Susan Kenfield declared. "You won't give me an abortion yourself, and—"

"You bet your sweet stupid life I won't!"

"—and you're trying to frighten me out of having someone else do it! Well, don't think I won't! Everyone's not as mean and beastly as you are."

"Why haven't you," said Doc, "found someone already?"

"I—none of your business," said Miss Kenfield, "I told you why, Murph, darling. I wouldn't trust any doctor but you."

"Why, Suzy?"

"Murph, you're getting tiresome, pet. Now be a sweet doctor and let me have a drink, mmm?"

"Why?" Doctor Murphy repeated.

She looked away from him nervously. After a moment, she moved her shoulders in a shrug of indifference. "Well," she said, still averting her gaze from his, "I just haven't, that's all."

"You did try another doctor, didn't you, Suzy? And he turned you down."

"We-ell . . ." Miss Kenfield shrugged again. "He was such a stupid man, Murph. He tried to tell me—"

"I've got a damned good idea what he told you," said Doctor Murphy. "When did you go to him? No, wait a minute. When did you first go to *a* doctor with this deal? How long ago?"

"Just—well, it was just before I started drinking this time."

"That was the last one you went to. I'm talking about the

first one. And don't tell me you—only went to one. Don't tell me you haven't been to every goddam abortionist in town!"

"Why, Murph!" Miss Kenfield widened her eyes in surprised innocence. "What in the world makes you think I—?"

"I don't know why in hell I didn't see it before," snapped Doc. "You came to me because the guys in the racket wouldn't touch the job with a ten-foot pole. They were afraid to. All right, Suzy, let's have it. And you'd better give it to me straight if you value that stupid life of yours. When—how many months ago—did you first try to get this abortion performed?"

"About—uh—about—" The actress bit her lip tremulously. "You won't be cross with me, darling? They were such sillies, Murph! Why, anyone could see I'm not—"

"Suzy!"

"I . . . about four months ago . . ."

"Four months!" Doctor Murphy literally howled. "You were too far along for an abortion four months ago, and yet you—you—!"

Offered sufficient inducement, any abortionist would have operated on Susan Kenfield up to the third month of pregnancy, and there were an incautious few who would have risked her life with an abortion at four months. But there were none so money-hungry as to abort a woman more than four months pregnant. So, Suzy must have been more than four months along—*four months ago!*

"Suzy," said Doc wearily. "I don't know why the hell I don't murder you."

"But, Murph! How could I possibly—?"

"You aren't the first woman not to show it. There was a college girl down in one of the coastal towns a few years ago. She had two babies without ever missing a class, and without even her parents getting wise. Killed 'em and buried 'em on a vacant lot."

Miss Kenfield shivered delicately. Doctor Murphy gave her a scornful glance.

"You wouldn't do that, would you? You're too damned good—like hell! Well, the hell with it. The hell with you.

You're eating lunch, and then you're getting out of here. I mean it, by God. Right this afternoon."

"Murph," wailed Miss Kenfield, "w-what will I do? I'll be ruined! Those filthy gossip columnists will find out, and I'll be kicked out of pictures, and—"

"If they were going to kick you out, they'd have done it long ago. This baby may be the very thing that'll keep you in. It'll take your mind off yourself, give you something to live for besides getting drunk."

"I'm s-so sick, Murph. So terribly sick."

"Yes," said Doctor Murphy, "and you're going—"

He broke off the sentence and stood up, stricken suddenly with the old, the inescapable feeling of self-guilt. She was an alcoholic. She'd come to him for help. And what had she got? Nothing. Nothing at all from the man whose specialty was treating alcoholics. Because he was an ignoramus, a failure.

"I'm sorry, Suzy," he said, quietly. "Just sit tight here until I can step down the hall and get my bag. I'll give you something to make you feel better."

"C-can I—could I have a drink, d-darling?"

"Not now."

"W-when?"

Doc shook his head. "That'll be a problem for your doctor. Do whatever he tells you to do."

"But"—Miss Kenfield looked up, her tear-stained face startled and hurt—"But, Murph. You're my—"

"Not any more, Suzy. After you leave here today, I'm not seeing you again."

He turned and walked out of the room, closing the door on her protests. Down the hall a few steps he unlocked the laboratory, and snapped open his worn leather medicine kit. He looked down into its contents, absently, wondering what was best to give Suzy. Wondering . . .

Wondering.

He heard Josephine's heavy shuffling tread in the hallway. It ceased, and he heard the scrape of a tray as it was braced against wood, and the turn of a doorknob. And then—

When he recalled it afterwards, it was as a nightmare, a hideous hag-ridden dream, enduring for years yet somehow packed into seconds. The terror struck so quickly, and yet lasted an eternity.

First there was a muffled whoop, then another, less muffled, and a third not muffled at all—completely unrestrained, gargantuan in its hysteria. They rolled out like shapeless off-key notes in some unearthly scale, each louder and higher than the other, mounting to their awful crescendo. They held there a moment; then they started down the scale again. And with them, minor notes in the unheavenly discord, were other sounds.

The wild clatter of dishes, silverware.

The metallic, reverberating thud of a tray.

And a scream—a scream that was part curse, part prayer, part frantic cry for help—from Susan Kenfield.

That's it, Doc thought. That did it. But the knowledge of what had happened, and its certain aftermath, was in its nightmarish way lacking intrinsic impact. It was the black norm in a black world. It had happened. It had had to happen. There was no escape from it. There was nothing to be done about it.

He saw that his hands were trembling, and that seemed not to matter either. Because there was nothing he could do or was going to do. He snapped the leather bag shut, closing each snap separately. He looked at the drop-end examination table, and it seemed only right and wise that he should raise the end of the table and stretch out. To let everything go—as it would go, anyway.

He didn't do it, of course; habit was too strong. But it was not sufficiently strong to dispel completely the nightmare's dead lethargic hand. It gripped his arms, slowing their motions. It clutched and dragged at his feet. Instinctively—instinctively since there seemed no reason to do so—he fought to shake it off. And the struggle angered him, and the anger helped.

He left the laboratory and went down the hall again. He pushed open Susan Kenfield's door and went in.

Josephine was bent over the bed, and her great body

obscured all of Suzy's except her two widespread, convulsively twitching ankles. He spoke to Josephine—laid a hand on her shoulder; and the hand was impatiently shrugged off.

Casually, he moved around to the other side of the bed.

Susan's eyes were wide open, but fixed in a trance-like somnolent gaze. A deep, gasping and throaty snore emerged from her gaping mouth.

Her hands were thrown back, locked tight around the bed rail.

Absently, Doctor Murphy watched the heaving and undulant torso. He watched the slow, steady dilation of the labia. Water, yellow and red streaked, was seeping through them. Very definitely, it wouldn't be long, now.

"Well"—Josephine was glaring at him—"you jus' goin' to stand there? Get some more sheets under her!"

"It's—it's all right about the bed," said Doc. "We mustn't do anything to disturb her."

Josephine grunted. The grunt tapered into a soothing croon, as she laid a hand on Susan's forehead.

"Don' you mind now, honey. Everything goin' to be all right. Ol' Josephine takin' care o' you, and she done midwived more babies'n you can shake a stick at. She . . . Doctuh, ain't you know nothin' to do *a-tall?*"

The exasperation of her voice was like the prick of a needle.

He nodded curtly and strode into the bathroom. He stoppered the sink and tub and turned on the hot water. He snatched a white metal tray from the bag, and emptied a flask of alcohol into it.

Scissors, a knife, forceps, clamps—no, no clamps; he'd never had any use for them. He dumped scissors, knife and forceps into the tray, then dug a quarter from his pocket and tossed it in also.

He scrubbed his hands, shook them dry and closed the water taps with his elbow.

He carried the tray into the bedroom, and received a grunt of approval from Josephine.

"All right," he said, shortly. "I'll take over."

"Says who?" inquired Josephine, but she chuckled. "This my line, doctuh. This all my family's line. Any takin' over to be done, reckon I better do it."

Doc hesitated, uncomfortably. Josephine chuckled again. "Don' you worry about me. I'm all washed good, an' I know 'zackly what else to do. You jus' get me all them towels out of the bathroom an'—*now*. Get 'em now!"

Susan Kenfield's body had risen from the bed in a sudden contortive thrust. The snoring sound changed to a low, moaning scream; and a flood of water, a pink tide gushed from her loins. And Doctor Murphy was into the bathroom and out again, seemingly without moving from his tracks. He was reaching under the thrusting thighs, wiping away the mess, mopping the vulva clean of its obscuring slime.

And Josephine laughed with gentle, chiding humor. "Got your han's all dirty again, ain't you? You reckon maybe I better cotch the baby?"

"Well—I—"

"Sho, now," Josephine grinned sympathetically. "This'n ain't goin' to be no trouble, a-tall. Mama like this'n it slide right out like a eel f'm a slippery elm. You want to do somethin' you rinse them towels out. We goin' to need 'em again."

Doc wasn't sure, but he had the impression later that he had argued with her. He had wanted to call Rufus; he had wondered profanely where Rufus was. He had wanted to call Miss Baker, another doctor, an ambulance. Or so, at least, was his later impression. But argument or no, he lost little time in following Josephine's suggestion.

He rinsed the towels out in the tub, pulled the stopper, and turned on the tap again. He hurried back into the bedroom.

Susan's moans formed a kind of rhythm now, a rhythm timed to the undulant heavings of her body. The distended and dilated labia formed an almost perfect circle, several inches in diameter. And a moist, round object was pressing its way slowly through the pink-rimmed periphery of the circle.

"Ain't I tol' you so?" breathed Josephine. "Jus' like a eel from a slippery elm."

Susan gave the greatest heave of all. She screamed, sobbed and was silent. And Josephine's hands dipped expertly—catching and lifting the baby away from the propelling outrush of afterbirth.

She shifted the baby onto one of her great work-worn palms. With the other, she swiftly fingered away the mucous from its mouth and nostrils. Then, she shifted it again, turned it on its stomach, and smacked it smartly on its red wizened bottom. And its red, wizened face puckered, and the tiny mouth opened and there was a kitten-like wail.

"Now, ain't he a dandy li'l man," said Josephine. "We just do him one l'il job, an'! . . ."

Doctor Murphy snipped the umbilical cord, placed the disinfected coin over the child's umbilicus and taped it into place. He didn't know that it was necessary; certainly, there seemed to be no indication of an incipient navel rupture. But it would do no harm, and it seemed imperative to do something. He had had practically nothing to do with the delivery. Susan, deep in the exhausted post-birth sleep, required nothing.

"You know," he confessed shakily. "It's a hell of a thing to admit, but that's about all I remembered. The coin on the navel, I mean."

"Suah," Josephine nodded seriously, "ain't never no harm in it. Mammy allus use a coin when she had one."

"Well"—Doc wiped his face with his sleeve—"I'll get an obstet—a baby nurse out here just as quickly as I can. I'm sorry to put you through all this, but if you can take care of—"

"No one put me through nothin'," said Josephine. "I jus' do it on my own. Now you skedaddle on out o' here—better lay down from the looks of you—an' I take care of everything."

The baby wailed again, and jerked in her palms. Josephine swayed it gently, nodding to the doctor. "I take care o' him," she said. "I take care o' her. You take care o' yo'self and everything be fine an' dandy."

His long legs dangling from the end of the laboratory examination table, Doctor Murphy shifted his position for perhaps the thousandth time in less than an hour, and at last abandoned the idea of resting. He wasn't tired—why the hell should *he* be tired? There was too much on his mind.

Josephine . . . She must have known all along that Suzy was on the point of giving birth. She must have to have moved as quickly as she had when Suzy's time came. She'd known exactly what to do. Probably—hell, there was no probably about it—she would have handled everything by herself if he hadn't shown up. Capably, without fuss or flurry. She'd known that the birth was going to be normal, that Suzy and the baby would be all right. She'd known everything that he was supposed to know, and hadn't.

Doc grinned wryly, watching the smoke squirm against the white walls of the laboratory.

Josephine, illiterate, superstitious, yet with more real knowledge of obstetrics than a top-flight practitioner. Josephine, reared in ignorance by the same civilization which would punish her so severely if she tried to practice her skill.

Josephine would never preside in a hospital delivery room. She would never be admitted to one even as a nurse. And it was too bad, a tragedy—but, well, life, God knew, was full of tragedies.

The General, with nothing to live for but drink and his impossible book.

Susan Kenfield, a great talent slowly drowning in booze.

The Holcombs, with so much of everything that they had nothing.

Humphrey Van Twyne, Bernie Edmonds, Lucretia Baker . . . all tragedies. All of them. Not to mention a certain doctor named Murphy who, being too stupid and stubborn to submit to the unchangeable, was the biggest tragedy of the lot.

The facts were before him, weren't they? He couldn't sacrifice Van Twyne without sacrificing the integrity which had got him into this spot. He couldn't simultaneously be a snide and a samaritan. You were either a quack—or you weren't. You had certain inviolable standards—or you didn't have. It couldn't be both ways. If you permitted yourself to condemn a man to almost certain idiocy, then you lacked the character to fight the battle of alcoholism.

Something inside you would be changed. No matter how you might rationalize and try to justify your actions, you'd lose something that you had to have.

Those were the facts. That was the situation, and it wasn't debatable. He had to do something that couldn't be done. If he intended to keep this place operating.

Doc slid from the table and walked to the sink, began dousing cold water over his face. Those were the facts, and yet, ridiculously, he couldn't bring himself to the only possible decision. He hadn't been able to this morning, and now with his success with Jeff Sloan—his seeming success, rather, since you could never be sure of anything when it came to alcoholics—he was further than ever from the decision. He almost wished that Jeff had . . . oh, hell, he didn't really wish it, but it would have made things a lot simpler.

It was strange how, the less you had to fight and hope for, the harder you fought and hoped.

He heard Josephine approaching, and he stepped back from the door, drying his face. She tapped on the panel and he called for her to come in.

"Well, Doc," he smiled, "how are our patients?"

"They doin' just fine," Josephine beamed. "Miz' Kenfield wake up an' get one look at'at funny li'l ol' chile, an' take him right into bed with her. Nurse can't get him away from her."

"Why—why that won't do." Doc frowned. "She ought to be resting, and the baby—"

"Baby ought to be with its mammy," said Josephine, "an' 'at's right where he is. An' don't you worry none about

Miz' Kenfield. 'At's one mighty strengthy woman, doctuh. She be alive an' kickin' long time after you an' me's dead an' gone."

"But it's unheard of for—"

"Who unheard of it? You know where I was bo'n, doctuh? Right out in the cotton patch. An' mammy went right on pickin' afterwards. Picked more'n three hunnerd pounds 'at day an' then she carried me back to the house, an' fix suppah for the fambly."

"That's a little different. Your mother was used to hard work, and—"

"Wasn't used to half o' what Miz' Kenfield is," said Josephine. "No, suh, mammy never be able to take what she taken. You shoot 'at li'l ol' Miz' Kenfield out o' a cannon, doctuh, I bet it don't even make a dent in her."

Doc laughed unwillingly. Suzy's activity, so soon after giving birth, seemed dangerously phenomenal.

"She want to see you, doctuh."

"Oh," said Doctor Murphy. "You said she was getting along all right. What does she want—something to drink?"

"Didn't ask for nothin'. Jus' wants to see you. She say you ain't goin' to have nothin' more to do with her, and it kinda make her feel bad."

Doc blinked. "Well," he said slowly, "all I meant by that was . . ." He paused, feeling for the moment the same stir of excitement that Jeff's promise to forswear drinking had given him. Suzy would never have a better excuse than she had now to drink—or stay sober; depending on whether she thought only of her own ordeal or the child that had derived from it. If she was going to pull herself together, she'd do it now or never. And since she hadn't asked for a drink—

Naturally, she hadn't asked Josephine for whiskey. Josephine, she knew, would have to ask him and he could deny the request without arguing about it. So, she was putting on this little act, pretending to be worried about his feelings toward her. And as soon as he stuck his bead in the door, she'd go into part two of the act.

No, they didn't change after they got as far along as Suzy.

Not when they were psychos as well as alcoholics. About all you could do was what he had announced doing earlier this afternoon: get her out of here as quickly as possible, and see that she stayed out.

"I'll see that she gets a drink," he said, "and I'll drop in on her a little later. Everything else okay? Rufus help you clean things up?"

"They all cleaned up," said Josephine. "Yes, suh, every thing okay."

"Rufus take care of the nurse? See that she has everything she needs?"

"Nurse all taken care of," said Josephine quickly. And Doctor Murphy misunderstood the shortness of her reply.

"I can't tell you how much I appreciate what you've done, Josephine. I wish I could—could do something in return, but the way things are now—"

"Sho, now" Josephine was embarrassed. "Ain't no call to feel 'at way. An', looky, doctuh . . ."

"Yes?"

"About money . . . I jus' soon you allus owe me some. It kinda give me my edge, you see? Me an' my crazy laughin' don't set too well with folks. They keep me around, they *givin'* me somethin'; they keep me owin' them. So . . . so me'n you, we keep even, huh, doctuh? You owe me somethin' an' I owe you."

Doctor Murphy grinned. "I'll be glad to oblige you, Josephine. Now, about the nurse. I know you're entirely capable of taking care of Miss Kenfield and her baby, but you have so many other things to do I—"

"An' I bettah start doin' 'em," said Josephine. "You want me to bring you some coffee or somethin', doctuh? Why'n't you go up to your room, an' I bring you a tray."

"Why"—Doc looked at her—"why, that's very nice of you, Josephine, but . . ."

She pulled the door open and nodded to him, made a small shooing motion with her hand. Doctor Murphy remained where he was.

"Josephine," he said, "Where is Rufus?"

"Rufus? He around somewhere. Now, you come along,

doctuh, an'—an'—well," said Josephine, and she edged through the door herself. "I bettah be gettin' busy."

"Where is he, Josephine? What's going on here?"

"Yes, suh," said Josephine. "Suah, got to be gettin' busy. Didn't ree'lize how late it was . . ."

The door closed after her.

Doctor Murphy rocked indecisively on his toes. He cast a weary, almost longing glance at the table. Why not? Why not let them all go their rotten irresponsible way, as, without knowing the details, he knew they were doing? They had the jump on him by almost two hours. With that much of a start, it would take days—days which he wouldn't have—to undo the damage.

Oh, he knew what had happened, all right. Just as, basically, there is but one major danger in a powder magazine, there is only one in a sanitarium for alcoholics. Rufus was still with them—all of them together in that one room. And they'd been too occupied with themselves to notice the noisy goings-on of the afternoon.

So it could be only the one thing. But, curiosity began to puncture Doctor Murphy's lassitude, curiosity and hope. Where had they got the stuff? And Rufus and Jeff: how could they—?

The answer, part of the answer, rather, came to him immediately. The Holcombs had used up their supply. No one had visited them and they, of course, hadn't been outside the sanitarium. So, it had had to come from in here. And there was only one person, aside from himself, who had a key to the liquor closet. Nurse Baker.

Doc cursed murderously. Goddam her—yes, and goddam Jeff Sloan! Jeff, his "success," the guy who wasn't going to drink any more. And Rufus, Rufus knew better than this. Rufus would know it was all wrong.

Nothing was to be expected from the others, but how could Jeff do this? Grab at the first drink that was offered to him.

"He didn't," Doc muttered, knowing full well that Jeff could and had. "Damn him, he just couldn't!"

And he left the laboratory, moved swiftly and silently down the hall.

He came to the Holcombs' door. Without breaking his stride, he entered the room. He stood there for a moment, just inside the door, before they became aware of his presence.

"Now, I insist," the General was saying. "Jeff, fix a drink for our good friend, Rufus. I insist that Rufus join us."

"Sure," said Jeff, busily mixing drinks at the dresser. "I'll take care of him."

"Not me. No, Suh." Rufus chuckled uneasily. "I ain't crazy. I'm jus' black."

Jeff grinned appreciatively and looked around, and his eyes met Doctor Murphy's. "Well," he said, "look who's here, guys. What kept you so long, Doc?"

Doc looked at him silently. He stared, tight-lipped, around the room, ignoring the General's genial greeting, the Holcombs' welcoming nods. Bernie Edmonds gestured to a chair.

"You're just in time, Murph. Jeff, what about a drink for Doc?"

"And Rufus," said the General. "Special occasion, y'know. Wouldn't be complete without Rufus."

"By the way, Doc," said John Holcomb, "what was all the rumpus about? Did Suzy finally go into d.t.'s?"

"I thought I heard a baby crying," said Gerald Holcomb. "Uh"—he laughed uncomfortably—"maybe you'd better give me a thorough check-up."

He looked at them one by one, weighing them and finding them hideously wanting. He looked down at the scuffed toes of his shoes, ridiculously in contrast with the waxed parquet floor. It was no wonder they thought they could get away with murder. It was no wonder that Miss Baker thought she could. He gave them a palace to live in; he treated them like kings—no, more than that, like friends. For them, he made a bum of himself, and who was to blame if they treated him like a bum?

Jeff cleared his throat "Look, Doc. I—you didn't mean for us to have this? Is that it?"

Doc shrugged. There was a vague, half-formed thought in the back of his mind, the entangled threads of several thoughts. *What was the occasion? Why wasn't Jeff apologetic about his backslide? How had they drunk so long with so little visible effect?* . . . But—to hell with all that. Beneath one of the beds, back against the wall, he could see the glint of two empty bottles. And Jeff was pouring from a full quart. That was all that mattered.

"Well, how about it?" Jeff demanded, frowning. "Don't just stand there, Doc. After all, we didn't ask for the stuff."

"But you couldn't turn it down, could you?" Doc spoke for the first time. "You couldn't do that, could you?"

"Now, that's hardly fair, Murph," Bernie protested. "I'm sure we're all sorry if Miss Baker acted without authority, but you can hardly blame a group of alcoholics for—"

"You're sorry," said Doc. "You're always sorry. You're not to blame. You never are. You sit in here guzzling all morning—you and Jerry and John. And Jeff—he gets drunk on his own, puts more away than you do. And the General, the only reason he doesn't get stiff is that he can't get out of bed. He doesn't lose any time as soon as he's on his feet. None of you ever misses a chance, and if you don't have a chance you make one. And then you're sorry, and you're not to blame. Well, skip it. I don't give a good goddam what you do."

He took out his key-ring, removed a key from it and tossed it to Rufus. "That's to the liquor closet," he said. "Ask Miss Kenfield how much she wants to drink, and give her whatever she asks. And bring back some more for our friends here. As much as they want."

Rufus scratched his head His white teeth gleamed in a bewildered, uneasy grin.

"You say what I think you did, doctuh?"

"I said it. You don't mind, do you? You can tear yourelf away from here for a few minutes? I'm sure these gentlemen will excuse you."

"I—uh, no, suh, I ain't got nothin' to do here. Just been kinda lookin' on. Didn't know quite what to do, so I just—"

"Well, now you know. Gentlemen? Is there anything else I can do for you?"

"You might sit down," said Gerald Holcomb, quietly. "Brother, can't you persuade the good doctor to be patient with us a little longer. I'm sure that when he understands all, he'll be inclined to forgive."

"I probably would," Doctor Murphy cut in "I'd probably wind up by pinning a medal on you. I'm stupid enough. So let's just save time and say that you can do as you please, get as drunk as you please, and it won't make a damned bit of difference to me. I'm through with you—through with this whole ridiculous, heart-breaking business. As of tomorrow, gentlemen, El Healtho will be no more. I've had enough."

There was a moment of stunned silence.

The General rose shakily from his chair. "But m-my book, doctor. What about my book?"

"That's your problem. You're all your own problems from now on, General."

"B-but—but we're—"

"Have fun," said Doctor Murphy, and he gave them an ironic salute.

Then, as they all started talking at once, as Jeff seemed on the point of exploding, he walked out and slammed the door.

That took care of them. Now, to take care of her.

He went up the steps, slowly, giving his anger time to build, focusing it on the lissome and lisping person who was its logical target. After all, while it was only natural to be disgusted and disappointed with Jeff and the others, to give them up as a hopeless job, it was childish to be angry with them. It was as foolish as it was futile to scold them for lacking will power. You might feel they could have resisted, if they'd really tried. But there you were posing a contradiction. Men don't resist the thing that has become all-important to them. They weren't accountable.

Miss Baker was.

Icy-eyed, his thin face flushed and taut, he strode down the mezzanine, and his rage grew with every step. She hadn't left yet, he knew. No cab had called at the sanitarium. And this fact, somehow, was the most maddening of all. The nerve of the dame! Telling him where to head in, feeding booze to his patients, and then hanging around! Thought she could get away with it, did she? Thought he'd be afraid to do anything.

He stopped in front of her door, listened a moment, and raised his fist. Then, grinning wickedly, be lowered it and took out his keys. He selected one, small and flat and multiple-notched, and slid it into the lock. Silently he turned it, simultaneously turning the knob.

He stepped inside, and—and he stopped. His Adam's apple traveled up and down his throat in an awed gulp.

Of course, he'd had an idea what she was like beneath that white starched uniform. He'd known she must be stacked like a brick back-house in windy country. But having an idea of what she was like, and seeing the reality—the *bare* reality—was something else again. So much so that Doctor Murphy felt a dangerous, almost paralyzing weakness creeping over him.

She was sprawled on the bed on her stomach, completely nude, a lush ivory-colored figurine. Her outspread legs, tapering up into perfect thighs, emphasized the flaring, pearshaped lines of her buttocks. Her firm full breasts pressed against the pillows, exaggerating the delicious curve of her back.

Doc gulped a second time. With an effort he tore his eyes away from her. Incuriously, a little dazed, he saw the half-packed suitcases, saw what appeared to be the remnants of a torn blouse and slip. Helplessly, he looked back at the bed again.

It was too much. That much in one dame—all that in five feet and a hundred pounds—well, it ought to be illegal.

He moved forward, grimly, slowly massaging the palm of his right hand against his trousers.

He came even with the bed. He raised his hand. He swung.

His open palm came down upon her bottom with an explosive, rifle-like *cra-aack!*

There was a smothered scream. Then, a louder one as Miss Baker's face came out of the pillow. She scrambled and stumbled to her feet, stood jiggling and swaying on the bed, at once trying to massage her pain-wracked posterior and to shield her body from his gaze.

Doc laughed contemptuously.

"Some fun, eh, Lucretia? Almost as much fun as giving whiskey to alcoholics."

"Y-you get out of here!" gasped Miss Baker. "You get out or I'll—I'll—"

He bent forward swiftly and grabbed at her ankle. Miss Baker stumbled back against the wall.

"G-get away! Y-you—you know she wouldn't let me leave! You know I don't dare to!"

"Who wouldn't? What the hell are you talking about?"

"Josephine. And don't tell me you didn't put her up to it!" Miss Baker gestured to her head and hastily lowered her hand again. "H-hitting me! T-trying to th-tab me! You know I—"

"You had it coming I'll bet. What'd you do to her?"

"Nothing! Not a thing—*help!*" screamed Miss Baker, for Doc's hand had closed around her ankle.

He dragged her forward, screaming and sobbing, clawing at the bedclothes.

She jerked and kicked herself free, flung herself back toward the wall. Doc cursed and made a dive for her.

"Now," he grunted. "Now, by God . . . !"

His strong hands pinned her arms. He jerked her around, holding her helpless against him. They lay there, panting, her sweet-smelling hair in his face, her breasts crushed against his chest, her legs locked and held by his.

She squirmed. She squirmed again. And Doc's arms suddenly became nerveless . . . There was no use in stopping now, of course. This was more than enough to wind him up permanently. Criminal assault. Assault with attempt to commit rape. It wouldn't make any difference now, so he might as well go ahead.

He might as well—but he couldn't do it.

He took a final half-hearted clout at her bottom, and started to rise. And Miss Baker wiggled frantically to escape the blow. And somehow—he was never quite sure how it happened—she was lying beneath him. All the soft, warm wonder of her body was cushioning his. And she was weeping in a curious, helpless way; and her fluttering, frantic hands seemed to caress rather than claw.

And the Doctor Murphy that was surrendered to the Doctor Murphy who had never been allowed to be—the Doc who had felt impelled to beat the dog-beater, jab the impudent waiter, collect from that little Bellevue teaser. That Doc—the one who had never been permitted to resolve a situation in the one satisfactory way possible—took over.

Miss Baker's eyes widened in sudden terror. They closed again, and her breasts arched and trembled with a kind of shivering sob. She gasped. She groaned.

She cried out, faintly.

. . . It was all over, seemingly, almost as soon as it began: So long had the submerged Doc been denied. Then, having had his way, he fled, leaving the other Doc—his cautious, safe and sane victim—to face the inevitable and horrendous music.

He sat on the edge of the bed, gloomy, shaky, sick with shame and foreboding. He couldn't bring himself to look at her. He couldn't speak. He could only sit and stare at the floor, stare, rather, into the future with its certain disgrace, a prison sentence, the loss of his license, the loss of everything.

Oh, she could do it all right. He wasn't exaggerating the seriousness of the situation. A virgin, just as he'd known she must be, and it wouldn't be any trouble at all to hang it onto him. It would be useless to fight, even if he had felt like fighting.

"Well," he said, at last, and waited. "Well, why don't you say something? Do something and get it over with."

Silence.

"Oh," he said. "Well, I'll get out. Then you can call the cops."

Silence still.

"I'll call them for you, if you like. I'll—do you want me to get you a doctor? I—"

"Thilly," said Miss Baker. "You thilly, thilly man! I already have a doctor."

Her arms went around him.

16

He was starting down the steps, moving in a blissful, pink-clouded glow, before the cold sun of circumstance again pushed into his horizon. Back there with her, everything had been simple. Now, seeing a sullen Rufus lingering at the bottom of the stairs, reality punctured the dream.

She mattered none the less to him, but she could not be the all of his world. In her, he had added one more complication to the hopelessly snarled skeins of his life. Nothing whatsoever had been solved.

He was broke. He was or soon would be a doctor without a practice. A doctor who had failed at the only thing he had ever wanted to do.

"Well"—he looked at Rufus coldly—"everyone getting nice and stiff?"

"No, suh, they ain't gettin' nice and stiff," said Rufus. "An' they ain't goin' to. I done picked up that bottle an' put it back in the closet, an' Miss Kenfield ain't drinkin' nothin' either. She say"—Rufus looked Doc squarely in the eye—"she say to tell you you just as stupid as you is ugly."

Doctor Murphy reddened. "I think," he began, sternly, "that you had better—" Then, the full impact of the Negro's words struck him, and he grasped Rufus by the shoulder. "Did you say that they—that she—?"

"Yes, suh," nodded Rufus. "I'm sorry about the baby, doctuh—I mean, not bein' on hand when you must have needed me. But I didn't know, an' . . ."

"To hell with that! How much did those guys have to drink this afternoon?"

"Just 'at one drink you saw. The one they was waitin' to have with you. Mistah Jeff, he didn't have none. Just fixed 'em for the General an' Mistah Bernie an' Mistah Holcomb."

Doctor Murphy stared, incredulously. "Now, wait a minute! I saw two empty bottles under the . . . oh," said Doc. "Of course."

"Yes, suh. Reckon them must've been old ones."

"But"—Doc spread his hands helplessly—"what's it all about? What were they all doing there together?"

"They talkin' about the book—how they goin' to make it into somethin' that is somethin'. Miz' Baker come in while they talkin', an' she say, Oh, 'at's fine, an' they can all have a drink, and she gives 'em that quart. She say she tell you the good news, an' you be right in, an'—" Rufus paused, reproachfully. "What you 'spect, anyway? What you 'spect me to do? She my boss. You always tellin' me to min' my own business, an' do what I'm told. You always fussin' about me buttin' in on things I don't know nothin' about."

"But the book," said Doc. "What book do you mean?"

" 'At book the General wrote. What you 'spect me to do, doctuh? Tell Miz' Baker she ain't doin' right? Run an' ask you if she is? They wasn't drinking nothin'. Just talkin' an' waitin' for you to come. Looked to me like 'at was what I'd better do. Don't do no nothin'—don't do no thinkin'. Just stay there an' wait for you."

"Rufus"—Doc hesitated. "I'm sorry, Rufus. You did exactly the right thing. Miss Baker—uh—Miss Baker acted a little thoughtlessly, and she owes you an apology, also. And you'll have it from her, Rufus. But—"

"Yes, suh?" Rufus looked at him anxiously. "Everything all right, then? You ain't goin' to close up the sanitarium?"

"I don't . . ." Doc turned away, leaving the sentence unfinished. He did know, of course. And he should have given Rufus and the others some warning before this. But as long as he had waited this long. "I want to know more about that book," he said. "Have Mr. Sloan come to my office, will you?"

"He waitin' for you there now, doctuh. You say you ain't really—?"

"I'll talk to you later," said Doctor Murphy, and he hastened across the dining room and entered his office.

Jeff was seated on the lounge, thumbing through a medical magazine. He arose as Doc came into the room, his boyish good-natured face set in an expression of defiant reproach.

"Boy," he said, "do you ever go off half-cocked! Just because you see a guy with a glass—"

"I know, I know! I've talked to Rufus." Doc dropped down on the lounge, drawing Jeff down with him. "Now, what's all this about the General's book?"

"Why we're going to go to town with it, that's what!" said Jeff. "Bernie's going to rewrite it, under the General's by-line, of course. And I'll do the promoting, and the Holcombs will handle the sale. On their own—outside of their agency. I'm telling you it's a natural, Doc! Everyone's heard of the General! With Bernie to put his stuff in shape, and the rest of us to push and peddle it, I'll bet we have a million-copy sale"

Doc nodded slowly. "You might, at that," he said. "I think you will. What I'm wondering is . . ."

"Yeah?"

"Why didn't I think of something like this myself. It's been right in front of me all along. I've watched the General sliding further and further downhill every day. I've watched the same thing happen to John and Gerald and Bernie. All essentially because of the lack of any real interest in life. And I didn't know what to do about it. I had all the pieces in my hands and I was too damned stupid to put them together. You, now, you're in here less than two days and you—"

"I saw it," Jeff shrugged. "Why not? I'm not outside the boat looking in. I'm right in there with the others. But I'll tell you something, Doc." He tapped Doctor Murphy on the knee. "Before a guy can see anything, he's got to have his eyes opened. He's got to want to see."

Doc shook his head. "I'm afraid you're giving me too much credit, Jeff. Naturally, I like to think that what I said helped, but I've talked myself blue in the face to hundreds of other patients. And for all the good it did, well . . ."

"How do you know it didn't do any good? How do you know it won't do some good eventually?"

"Well . . ."

"I'll tell you the way I see it, Doc. It's kind of like my game. You call on a guy with a proposition, and maybe you hit him with exactly the right line at the right time, like you did me, and he goes for it. But the chances are that you won't. You have to keep pounding at him, day after day, and even then you miss out on the deal. But that doesn't mean, Doc, that absolutely doesn't mean that you haven't done any good. He'll remember you, if you've done your job right. He'll pick you up on your deal later, or maybe he'll mention you to a friend who is ripe for your proposition."

Doc sighed, and shifted on the lounge.

"The point is, Jeff, that I don't know my job. Not in anything resembling the way that you know yours. It's all pretty much hit or miss, shooting in the dark. You don't know where to aim or what to aim with."

"So?" said Jeff. "What's the difference? You just aim at and with everything."

"Jeff, you just don't understand."

"Yes, I do, Doc," said Jeff earnestly. "I can be a pretty lousy bastard when I'm drinking, but there's nothing wrong with my head—yet. You asked me earlier today why I'd decided not to drink any more, and I couldn't tell you. Now, I can. It's because you believed I could and would stop."

"Yes?" Doctor Murphy turned on him sharply. "How do you figure that?"

"You believed I could and you believe these other patients can. You're sure that eventually you can get them back on the track. Don't you see, Doc? You have to believe or you wouldn't be doing what you are. You wouldn't have gone into this kind of practice in the first place."

"Umm," said Doc. "And what if I'm all wet for believing that way?"

"But you know you're not. Everyone else might think so, even the alcoholic himself may have given himself up as hopeless. But you don't. You stay right in there pitching, giving it everything you've got, because you believe you're going to win out. Do you see how important that is Doc, to have someone to believe in you? Do you see how it would be if you gave up—if you stopped believing along with everyone else?"

Doc grimaced wryly. "You aren't a very hard-bitten case, Jeff. You might have made the decision to stop drinking by yourself."

"Leave me out of it, then. What about the others? I feel that I've got to know them pretty well today—better than you, maybe, because they'll let their hair down with another drunk. You can't give up now, Doc, just when you're on the point of succeeding. Those guys would hit the bottom and keep right on going."

"You think, then"—Doc's tone was deliberately cynical—"that they'll be all right, now? They won't drink any more, and the prince will marry the princess, and they'll all live happily forever after?"

"I think," said Jeff, "that they're nearer to being permanently sober than they've ever been before. I think they've stopped sliding and started climbing. I think they'll start sliding fast if you throw in the sponge here."

"Well . . ." Doc spoke the one word, and was silent.

"They were pretty badly upset, Doc. I told them you didn't mean what you said, that everything would be all right as soon as you understood what had happened."

"Did you?"

"I did," said Jeff. "Look, Doc"—he frowned—"what gives with this Miss Baker, anyway? Why did she give them that booze? Why crack down on the boys because of something she did?"

"That was my fault," said Doc curtly. "Miss Baker has been ill, and I knew it. She should be all right from now on."

"Well." Jeff looked at him puzzledly. "I guess I don't get it, Doc. Everything's fine, and yet you—you—"

Doctor Murphy leaped to his feet.

"I've had enough, get me? That's what's the matter. It's just been one goddam headache after another, and now I can't take any more. You've heard the news about Suzy Kenfield? Well, that's a small sample of what I've been up against ever since I opened this place. She might have died. The baby might have died. And all because she didn't and doesn't give a damn about anything so long as she can stay sozzled. I tell you—"

"We all went in to see the baby," said Jeff. "Miss Kenfield said she'd never felt better in her life."

"Sure. The damned selfish bitch is indestructible, but I'm not! I—"

"We were there," said Jeff, "when Rufus offered her the whiskey."

"All right," he said. "I've worked for years without making an inch of headway, and now everything's popping at once. Of course, it may all be a fluke, but I don't think so."

"You know it isn't, Doc."

"All right, I know it. And I wish I didn't. It would be easier if I knew that I'd failed. It would have been better for my patients if I'd done a complete flop. As it is, well just when they're getting their foot on the ladder I yank it out from under them."

"But, Doc—why?"

"You know why, Jeff. I can't do that to Van Twyne. I wouldn't be any good as a doctor if I did do it."

"But," Jeff hesitated uncertainly, "I know how you feel, but you didn't have your mind made up then when you took me up to see him. You were undecided then, when you didn't have any real reason to go on here, and now that you do have—" He paused again, looking down at the floor uncomfortably. "I'm not trying to talk you into it, understand."

"I can't do it, Jeff. I've known all along that I couldn't. So long as I had any time at all left, even a few hours, I ducked the facts. I've tried to kid myself that there was some other way out. Now, my time's run out and I know there isn't any other way. It's that way or none, so it has to be none."

"Well," said Jeff. "I—well," he repeated.

"Yes," said Doc, "I've screwed it up good. It's pretty generally known that I was having a hard time financially, but no one's known how bad things really were. Alcoholics are sensitive as hell. The majority of my patients are on their uppers. I was afraid that if I told them the truth, they'd hesitate about coming to me. So I've just gone on, getting in deeper and deeper, and now . . ."

"You're sure there isn't some way, Doc?"

"I've told you."

"Positive?"

"Dammit," said Doctor Murphy, "how many times do I have to tell you? Van Twyne was my only chance. That was why he was brought here, get me?"

"No," said Jeff, blankly, "I don't."

"His family's got a finger in every financial pie on the West Coast. Real estate, banks—every damned thing. They looked around for a good reputable sanitarium to bury Humphrey in, and when they came to mine they stopped looking. They knew how much this place meant to me. They knew I had to have big dough right away, or else. And they knew that if I didn't get it from them, I just wouldn't—" Doc paused abruptly. His eyes narrowed. "If I didn't get it from them," he murmured. "If I did get it from them, and . . ."

"Yeah, Doc?"

"Nothing," said Doc.

"That's a pretty dirty thing to do to you, Doc. Forcing a choice like that on you."

"Yes," said Doctor Murphy. "I thought it was myself."

He slapped the cigarette ash from his knees, and stood up. Hands jammed in his pockets, he stood in front of the window, looking down across the shrubbery and gardens and lawn to the highway.

A car was turning into the driveway at the foot of the slope. The afternoon sun sparkled blindingly on its long black hood, and the chrome flashed and sparkled like the dazzling, limitless millions which in a way it represented.

Doctor Amos Perthborg was arriving. Doctor Perthborg, physician to the Van Twyne family.

Doc turned away from the window.

"You'll have to excuse me now, Jeff."

"Sure," said Jeff, and turned slowly toward the door. "I hate to keep asking you, Doc, but are you dead sure there isn't some way to—?"

"The Van Twynes. That's the only way."

"Shall I—what shall I tell the guys, Doc?"

"Don't tell them anything. Tell them I was too busy to see you."

"But, Doc, that's—"

"You heard me," said Doctor Murphy, and he drooped a lid over one bright blue eye. "Now, get the hell out of here."

Long, long before, when a youngster with the impossible name of Pasteur Semelweiss Murphy was still in knee pants, the annual income of Dr. Amos Perthborg was approaching the six-figure mark. Not, you will understand, because his practice was a particularly large one. And not—very definitely not—because of his excellence as a physician. It was, rather, because of an attribute which many claim, but which, happily, very few possess: the trait of making no move which did not somehow contribute to his personal advancement.

Among his unsuspecting friends and associates, and they were, in the main, unsuspecting, Doctor Perthborg was regarded as whimsically eccentric, a man guided by his heart rather than his head. And to those whose looking-ahead was limited to days and weeks, instead of Doctor Perthborg's year and decades, it did often seem that he was. So easily is the straightforward disguised by complex society. So easily is the straight path confused with the ambling terrain it traverses.

During the economic depression, Amos Perthborg had lent thousands of dollars to beginning practitioners—lent it without note or collateral and often at the necessity of borrowing himself.

At a time when his own professional position was none too secure, he had boldly denounced the president of the county medical society as an incompetent fee splitter—which, though it is hardly pertinent, the president was.

Compared to the supplicant young doctors he had literally

booted out of his office, the ones he had aided comprised a mere handful. And these, a thoughtful observer (had such there been) would have noted, had been selected more for their catholicity than, say, precocity There was a heart man, an orthopedist, a gynecologist, a pediatrician, a brain surgeon, an eye-ear-nose-and-throat specialist . . . and so on. They were good but not brilliant men; Doctor Perthborg distrusted brilliance. As consultants, they had proved useful and lucrative for a great many years; not only by doing the work he was paid to do for a fraction of his fee, but in stamping his flagrant and sometimes fatal errors with their professional approval.

As for the president of the medical society, he had been old and the old lose the will to fight, and it is a basic principle of elementary politics never to vote no on a moral issue. The incumbent had been booted out of his post. Doctor Perthborg, elected by acclamation, virtuously refused the honor. His purpose had been accomplished, he said; he did not care to profit by it.

He did profit by it, needless to say. He had received hundreds of thousands of dollars worth of free advertising, and he winnowed the results carefully, narrowing them down to the choicest, fiscally strongest clientele. Moreover, having scared the daylights out of any competition, he and his proteges were left with practically a clear field in the consultant racket. Only for a time, of course, greed being eternal and fear ephemeral. But a very good time it was. It was during this period that Doctor Perthborg began his long association with the Van Twyne family.

Barbara Huylinger D'Arcy Van Twyne had got herself pregnant. Doctor Perthborg's consultants consulted with Doctor Perthborg and agreed that she could not give birth without serious risk to her life. She should, in other words, be aborted. She was. Whereupon she reassumed the many duties incumbent upon a champion woman golfer, tennis player, swimmer and high diver.

That, as has been noted, was the beginning of the Van Twyne-Perthborg association. The ending . . . ah, the ending.

Just where, Doctor Perthborg had begun to wonder, would the ending be?

You had moved in a straight line, and got to where you were going. The men you had moved to move yourself now approached your own stature, and far from being disturbed you were pleased and gratified. You were friends, insofar as you were capable of friendship. They wanted nothing from you, nor you from them. There was no past.

That was you, then, after three score of your allotted three and a half: portly in a purely comfortable way, comfortably active, comfortably rich. You had got what you wanted—wealth, position, family. You had moved in a straight line to worry-free, honorable comfort.

And a beady-eyed old witch, ancient yet seemingly ageless, who had not got all that *she* wanted—and never would, damn her!—came along and booted you in the tail. And you couldn't plead with her because there was nothing to appeal to, and you couldn't reason with her because she wouldn't argue. You could only move in the direction she indicated.

Seated across the desk from Doctor Murphy, Doctor Perthborg looked unhappy and was considerably unhappier than he looked. He had a feeling that however things turned out, the result for him would be disastrous. Yet there was nothing to do but go ahead. If he did not, if he so much as caviled—that was her word—the disaster would be immediate.

Doctor Perthborg beamed and nodded at Doctor Murphy, edging politely toward the subject of his visit. But, actually, he did not see Doc; his mind's eye was turned on the image of her—hawk-nosed, bitter mouthed, beady-eyed. A dried-up witch of a woman, perched in a chair that was like a throne, imperious, far more wealthy perhaps, than her namesake.

But my dear Victoria! You honestly can't expect me to—

I've told you what I expected. And don't dear-Victoria me, you sanctimonious old fake. You make me sick to my stomach!

But—but it's completely unethical! in a sense, it's murder.

Surely you wouldn't want your own grandson murdered.

I'd like nothing better. Unfortunately, I'm compelled to think of the publicity.

I can't—I won't do it!

Very well.

What . . . w-what will you do, Victoria?

About you? Well, I believe we are not dissimilar in character. What would you do, Amos—if you were in the position to do what I can?

. . . Doctor Perthborg removed his pince-nez, and rubbed them against the lapel of his two-hundred dollar suit. He reaffixed them on his nose and leaned forward, folding his fleshy face into a sympathetic mask.

"And Humphrey," he said. "How is the poor boy, Doctor?"

"Would you like to see him?"

"Oh, no, no, not at all," Doctor Perthborg protested. "That won't be necessary. I have complete confidence in you, Doctor?"

"Why?" said Doctor Murphy.

"Uh—why?"

"Sure. Why? I'm a psychiatrist with a limited g.p. practice."

"You underestimate yourself, Doctor. I've had glowing reports on your ability."

"Ability as a brain surgeon?"

Doctor Perthborg's lips compressed, his cheeks puffed out, and for a moment he resembled nothing quite so much as an angry toad. Somehow, however, he managed to smother his annoyance. He spoke to Doctor Murphy kindly, though on a note of gentle reproof.

"Love," he intoned, "that's what our boy needs, Doctor. After all—and I know you're not the ignoramus in these matters you pretend to be—what else can be done for him? How many lobotomy cases are ever able to resume normal lives, even under the skillful care of the world's greatest specialist? Not many, eh? We know the record of the specialists, Doctor—many failures, few, ah so pitifully few successes. So let's do it our way, the way of heart and soul. Let's keep the boy here in the bosom of his family, and give him . . ." Doctor Perthborg paused, icily. "Am I amusing you, Doctor?"

"I was never," said Doctor Murphy, "less amused in my life. Admittedly, the recovery ratio on pre-frontals is tragically low. As a psychiatrist, I don't feel that the operation is ever warranted. However—"

"We had no alternative, Doctor."

"I'm not sure that I agree, but let that pass. Humphrey went through the operation. Now, he's entitled to a chance. The only place he can get it is where the lobotomy was performed. The Paine-Gwaltney clinic in New York."

"I disagree, Doctor."

"No," said Doctor Murphy, "you don't. But we'll let that pass, too. We have some pretty good local men. Specialists. Let me call one in."

"No," said Doctor Perthborg.

"Let me call in a non-specialist, then. Any reputable practitioner."

"No."

"No," Doctor Murphy nodded, grimly. "You can't have a quack presiding at Humphrey's funeral; sooner or later, there'd be one hell of a scandal. You have to have a good man, and no one that's any good would touch the case."

"Come, Doctor." Doctor Perthborg smiled firmly. "A good man *has* touched the case. Yourself. One of the best, down-to-earth physicians we have in this blessed state. Frankly, I'm a little surprised, even disappointed, at his attitude, this belaboring of the inevitable. I had every reason to feel, it seemed to me, that we were pretty much in agreement on—"

"You took me by surprise," Doctor Murphy nodded. "And I don't mind saying that the proposition was tempting. It's either that, or give up my work here, and—"

"Very valuable work, Doctor. Important. Vital."

"I think so. So I'm probably much more sorry than you are to say what I have to. I don't want the case. Either you have Humphrey removed from here at once, or I will."

"B-but"—Doctor Perthborg turned pale—"I c-can't! You can't do that, Doctor!"

"Why can't I? What's to prevent me from sending him to the county hospital?"

"The *county!*" Doctor Perthborg got a grip on himself. "Doctor, is it—I thought we were being quite generous, but —is it a question of money?"

"It's a question of responsibility. Either I share it with someone—someone with a good professional reputation—or it's no deal."

"But you've already said that no one who was—uh, did you have someone in mind, Doctor? I'm not sure that the idea would be agreeable to Mr. Van Twyne, but if you could suggest someone of your own discretion . . ."

"Can you?"

"I? Ask one of my associates to—to—!"

Doctor Murphy grinned at him. "Too good for that, huh? They're too good. But I'm not."

"No, no! It's just that I don't know of anyone who meets the necessary qualifications. But if there's anyone you can—"

"I was hoping," said Doctor Murphy, "that he would suggest himself. In fact, I was so sure he would that I took the liberty of having this prepared."

He turned over the sheet of paper on his desk and pushed it toward Doctor Perthborg. The doctor picked it up, gingerly.

"Ummm"—he cleared his throat—"I feel that this is superfluous, Doctor. Entirely unnecessary. Obviously—by implication, that is—Mr. Van Twyne was placed in your care with my full approval. There could be no question in the mind of anyone that you were acting without authority."

"But you don't care to make it a matter of record?"

"But it *is* a matter of record! The check for your fee constitutes a record!"

"Not in my book, it isn't," said Doctor Murphy. "The implications are all one-sided. For fifteen thousand dollars, I give an implied promise to help Humphrey. I promise something and accept payment for something which I can't possibly deliver. You and the Van Twynes are in the clear. You accepted my professional word—mine alone

—and I let you down. Huh, uh, Doctor Perthborg. Not for me."

"Now, Doctor. You know we haven't the slightest intention of . . ."

"You haven't now, no. But it's not hard to imagine what you'd do if it was a case of your necks or mine."

"But this"—Doctor Perthborg looked down, unhappily at the paper—"the wording of it, Doctor: 'As the duly authorized physician to Humphrey Van Twyne III (incompetent), and having thoroughly examined and studied the aforementioned patient, I am in complete agreement with, and hereby agree to, the recommendations made by Dr. Pasteur Semelweiss Murphy, consulting physician-in-charge . . .' "

"Well?" said Doctor Murphy.

"What recommendations? What am I agreeing to? I can't go out on a limb like this!"

Doctor Murphy shrugged. "Well, let's re-word it then. Be specific. Give me your ideas on what should be done for Humphrey."

"But I don't know—"

Doc grinned at him.

Doctor Perthborg sighed.

Reluctantly, he uncapped his fountain pen and scrawled his signature at the bottom of the page.

"There you are, Doctor. And here's your check. You'll notice I've had it certified."

"Very thoughtful of you," murmured Doctor Murphy.

"So if you'll just sign this receipt . . ."

Doctor Murphy leaned back in his chair. Hands clasped behind his head, he stared thoughtfully up at the ceiling.

"You know, I've been thinking, Doctor. Establishments such as mine are always somewhat suspect, so I've been thinking . . ."

"Yes?" said Doctor Perthborg shortly.

"Well, the Van Twyne philanthropies are well known, and it's only logical that the family should have a deep interest in alcoholism. That being the case, and assuming that this situation has a strong potential for unpleasantness, suppose I accept that check as a donation rather than a fee?"

Doctor Murphy continued to stare at the ceiling. He was afraid to look away from it; certain that Doctor Perthborg would take one cold, calculating glance at his face and read the plan that was in his mind.

He waited—for hours it seemed. The silence became unbearable. Then, he heard a slow, thoughtful exhalation, and the squeak of a chair.

And the brief scratching of pen against paper.

"An excellent idea," said Doctor Perthborg. "I think the one word will cover it, don't you?"

Doctor Murphy thought it would. He was sure—ha, ha — that it would. Just the word 'Donation' across the corner of the check. That—ha, ha—that would take care of everything.

Doctor Perthborg looked at him with cynical amusement. He shook hands, and said good-day.

And as he drove away, he permitted himself a scornful and wondering laugh . . . The pitiful damned fool. Practically going into hysterics when he got his hands on that fifteen thousand! Why, if he'd been half the man that he, Doctor Perthborg, was, he'd have put on the squeeze for two times fifteen thousand!

Meanwhile, Doctor Murphy remained in his office. He remained at his desk, staring rather dazedly at the check.

There it was. He'd never thought he could get away with it. He felt unnerved, exhausted—wanting to yell with sheer relief yet lacking the energy to do it.

The check rattled in his trembling fingers, and he dropped it hastily. He gulped and brushed at his eyes . . . Fifteen grand! The sanitarium could coast a long time on that. And Humphrey Van Twyne would have his chance—the one in a thousand chance for normality, usefulness, happiness.

But it had been too much. He had given everything he had to get this far, and this far was really nothing. As yet he had done nothing. The last conclusive step was yet to be taken. A step across the abyss . . . or into it.

The door opened and closed gently. Miss Baker came firmly across the room.

"Ith there . . . ith there anything I can do, Doctor?"

"I don't know." Doctor Murphy barely looked up. "I mean, no, I guess not. Just thinking. Trying to think something through."

"If ith . . . I hope it doethn't conthern what I thaid about Jothephine. She's really a very sweet perthon, and I thimply mithunderthtood what she wath—"

"No," said Doc. "Josephine's all right."

"Mithter Thloan? Did he tell you? I put a full glath of whithkey in hith room today right after lunch."

Doctor Murphy glanced at her sharply. Then he shrugged. "So? It doesn't matter. Everything's all right now. You. Sloan. The General. Bernie. The Holcombs . . ." Doc laughed tiredly. "I don't know how the hell it happened, because I've been a bigger damned fool than usual. But everything's all right. Everything and everyone, but—"

"Yeth, Doctor?"

Doc shook his head.

Of course, they didn't want publicity, and there'd certainly be plenty if they decided to get tough. They'd be shown up for the rotten bunch of stinkers they were. There'd be a scandal that would make Humphrey's past exploits seem like Sunday school stuff . . . So the odds were all that they wouldn't do anything. They'd take their licking, and the day might even come—if Humphrey turned out okay—when they'd thank him for it.

But . . . but you could never be sure which way an outfit like that would jump. The fact that it was against their interests to kick up a fuss didn't mean that they might not do it. Undoubtedly, there was a strong streak of nuttiness in the entire family. If they got sore enough, they could make him wish he'd never been born. They could get his license pulled, hound him from place to place, break him and keep him broken. And the fact that they'd be in the soup too wouldn't help him any.

He didn't think they'd do it. They were too damned selfish, too shrewd to hurt themselves to get at another. But he couldn't be sure—he didn't *know*. And he wouldn't know until it was too late to back up.

Suddenly, he was almost terrified.

"Doctor . . ." She was looking down at the check, now, and somehow she seemed to know. She already knew he was a damned fool, and the check was enough to fill in the picture. "You crathy man," she breathed. "You know you're crathy?"

She moved unbidden to the filing cabinet. She consulted a white address card, and returned to the desk.

"Thath the Paine-Gwaltney Clinic, Forest Hills, New York . . . Straight telegram, Doctor?"

"Straight telegram," said Doctor Murphy, and he dictated. " 'Returning Humphrey Van Twyne your care. Also air-mailing photostat of carte-blanche authority from Van Twyne agent. Urge you spare no expense.' . . . How many words is that, Lucretia?"

"Nineteen, counting Van Twyne ath one word. Shall I try to cut—"

"Add two," said Doctor Murphy. " 'Good luck . . .' "

The long sanitarium day was ended. Ex-corpsman Judson had ascended the long stairs from the beach, and the great kitchen of El Healtho was dark and silent, and in their quarters Josephine and Rufus slept the sleep of the just.

In the double room of the Holcomb brothers, the General remarked that chronically opposed as he was to leaving pleasant company, he would have to ask to be excused: for the first time in years, he was honestly sleepy. And John stated that, oddly enough, he and brother also felt like sleeping. And Bernie and Jeff confessed to the same almost-forgotten sensation, and they all smiled at one another, happily, and said goodnight.

In her room, Susan Kenfield said, "Kitchy-koo, you darling, lovely, adorable, hideous little bastard," then she released him to the somewhat shocked nurse and peacefully closed her eyes.

In Room Four, Humphrey Van Twyne urinated in his winding sheets, and for a moment there was a flicker of intelligence in the chiseled white mask of his face. Eons, ages ago, there had been a void, black, empty, awesome, and then there had been this sudden wet warmth. And then? Then?

On the rear terrace, looking down upon the phosphorescent highway of moonlight which stretched endlessly into the Pacific, Miss Baker said she just knew everything would be all right, and Doctor Murphy said, well, he thought so too, and it'd damned well better be.

"We have a new patient, Doctor. I think you'd better see him."

"Bad?"

"Pretty well into delirium. Beaten up and rolled, apparently. I had to pay his cab fare."

"Damn! Okay, I'll be right with you." He ran to catch up with Judson.

"Better rig up a saline drip . . . What's his name, anyway? His job?"

"Couldn't quite get his name, Doctor. But he was babbling something about being a writer."

"Well, we'll wash out his bloodstream, get him back to work as soon as possible. That's what all these birds need. Something to keep—grab him!"

They grabbed him together, the puke-smeared, wild-eyed wreck who staggered suddenly into the corridor. He struggled for a moment, then went limp in their arms sobbing helplessly.

"T-tomcats," he wept. "S-sonsbitches t-thirty-four f-feet tall an' . . . n' got eighteen tails, n' . . . n' . . ."

"Yeah?" said Doctor Murphy.

". . . n' oysters for eyeballs."

Doctor Murphy chuckled grimly. "Yes, sir," he said, "we'll knock him out, wash him out, and get him back to work. I've got a job all picked out for this character."

"A job? I don't—"

"C-cats," sobbed the writer. "N' every damn one a lyric s-soprano . . ."

Doctor Murphy regarded him fondly. "A grade-A nut," he said. "A double-distilled screwball. Just the man to write a book about this place."